After hours of making slow motion love, after the mutual exchange of love feelings, he, the man, stood up and backed away from her, smiling, leaving her with a perfect memory.

She didn't feel the urge to know him beyond the point that they had been together. It had been perfect, no need to spoil it with any emotions beyond the ones they had shared.

Malana seemed to flow back into Valonga's field of vision, her body steaming from a brief dip in the river.

"A world of caution, Valonga, you can get what you wish here, if the vibe is right."

Valonga slowly opened her eyes and stared through the porthole above her bed. Juan Rojo Diablo was the man she had made love to, on her fantasy—dreamtrip—with Malana, the Braider. She felt absolutely certain that he was the man.

BRAZILIAN NIGHTS

ODIE HAWKINS

Originally published by Folio Graphics Co., Inc.

Copyright © 1992, 2012 by Odie Hawkins

Front cover photo by Zola Salena-Hawkins, www.flickr.com/photos/32886903@N02

ISBN: 978-1-5040-3581-1

Distributed in 2016 by Open Road Distribution
180 Maiden Lane
New York, NY 10038
www.openroadmedia.com

BRAZILIAN NIGHTS

Prologue

Te Loca, Moraes, Themba, Raheb, Far-I, Jumoke, The Bey, others, came to the loft on San Pablo in Oakland. The loft was supposed to be in the neighborhood it was in; the video of Cedric's at Mestre Bimba's school in Bahia, tells us that. Or maybe its only a vicious simile.

Valonga, this orphan named creature who floated down windblown streets on strips of fortune teller cookie paper, this unknown woman who suggested cosmic thoughts, couldn't do anything better than become a student of the world's masters.

What was she to do, what is there for any of us to do but grab this flare and lite it? Pity those whose flares have not been lit, have floated around in the darkness, unable to conquer ego and learn something.

Capoeira Regional (Hay-jonal) is new to this country (North America, U.S.A.), but Capoeira Angola hasn't been thought of. Regional is what Macumba is, a relation to Angola, in relation to Angola, in relation to Candomblé. Hear the deeper sounds and rhythms?

Valonga is the soul of those of us who want to crawl inside culturally based legacies and eat them. Valonga is the name of a sensitive orphan, a woman who was not given "traditional training." It did her all the good in the world. The World. Now we're getting somewhere. The world...

Lots of people in the world, they have different names, they do different things, they have different customs, they do different things. We're all basically fucked up, but some of us have learned to put a title on it.

"Fucked up 101" should be in every junior college brochure, it would make the learning process easier. Or maybe it would be better to skip 101 altogether and get out into the world, to see it for what it really is.

In every Explorer's heart there lurks the spirit of the Need To... maybe we should stop there because those who buy into the Spirit of the Need To don't need to have themselves explained to themselves, but for the others, "Fucked up #101."

Steady, but spontaneous. Hours, days, months, years pass before it is possible to become steady, but spontaneous. A lot of people don't believe it's possible to suture those elements. Valonga wanted to create a dream book, suture those elements, run her life into an uncontaminated spring. How many of us have ever paid any attention to the lives of the corn of cotton farmers we've passed through? Questioned the matadore about his reason for Being? Played with rhythm 'til it got home?

Why would anyone want to do these things? Why would a young African-American woman want to ease away from her turf, seek heart riffs more guttural than aches? But this is purely playing on words, the real stuff is piled up behind us.

Why? Why? Why? is the question-word Valonga Prince, of the Princes of Augusta, Georgia, heard from her earliest years.

"Why, Valonga? Why would you black that po' little boy's eyes like that?"

"'Cause he didn't show me the proper respect."

"We could've told his mother if he had called you a nigger, or something, they're civilized white folks. Did he call you a nigger?"

"Jeff Davis? Nawww, he'd never think of calling me a name."

"So explain why you blacked his eyes."

"I just told you, he didn't show me the proper respect."

"So, you thought that blacking his eyes would make him show the proper respect?"

"Nope, that was his idea. If I hadn't blacked his eyes he would've spent years thinking that he had a good defense system. I think I did him a favor."

Valonga, in her subteens, wanted to skin the world back, do the undoable. Esoteric stuff glared at her, forced her to ask questions that few people she knew had an answer for.

"Dad, why should Sumo wrestlers be so huge?"

"Mom, do we have a martial art, Africans?"

"Miss Phillips, why does the drum make us feel like that?"

"Mr. Beck, if all the races of the world are evolutions from the birthplace of the human being, how do we get Japanese?"

As she grew older and more penetrating, some people ducked when they saw her coming, the braver ones stood their ground and were bowled over.

"Who is responsible for the idea of a Superior Being? Does that have something to do with the Europeans trying to gain control of the Earth?"

9

"No, of course not."

"Then why are there so many European representations of Jesus, the Son of God?"

Tastebuds grew in her hands, beautiful sounds magnetized to her ears, her skin became an antennae. She decided to check the world out, seek out the wiser heads, glean as much as she could. Brazil seemed a good place to begin.

Chapter 1

The Bahian night throbbed with slurred sounds, musical wings flurried from a distant Candomblé ceremony, the echo-twang of a lonely Berimbau mounted the fragrant air.

Valonga sprawled on her narrow bed, bare from the waist up, a film of perspiration coating the narrow valley between her full breasts.

Bahia, Africa, San Salvador, Bahia, Brazil.

She laced her hands behind her basket woven braids and closed her eyes, soaking in the smells and sounds. So warm and humid, funky. She reached over to a bedside table for a half empty bottle of beer, her hand performing a languid search. She swigged from the bottle, poured a few drops of her breasts and indulgently massaged the liquid into her skin.

The chants and drums seemed closer. She took another swig of the warm beer and slowly replaced the bottle on the table. Bahia, Brazil. She re-laced her hands behind her head,

11

turned to stare out of her second floor window. Even the moon looks more sensual down here. She smiled at the thought and spread her legs wider.

"Valonga, what're you going to do down there?"

"I'm going to study the dynamics of Capoeira Angola."

"Girl, you don't know what to do with yourself, do you?"

"Of course I do, I've always known what to do with myself." Her smile broadened. Life was so sweet when people would take off for 3 years to explore their fantasies, do as much of what they felt they wanted to do. She took another sip from the bottle. Two weeks ago I was in Georgia, home, and now I'm in Bahia and it feels more like home than Georgia ever felt. She made a quick review of her mental tape, something she often did then she wanted to put her life in perspective.

Valonga Prince, of the African-American Princes of Augusta, Georgia, the founder and president of SMI ("The stress management consultants for international corporations"), the person she had designed herself to be.

"I think its silly that we should play follow the leader. Everyone is a leader if they're willing to take on that responsibility."

The way had been paved by a $300,000 inheritance from a hardworking father and a more than slightly bohemian mother.

"Go for it, Valonga, whatever the hell it is! That's what me and your Daddy did."

She had taken her mother's advice on more than one occasion and multiplied her inheritance a couple of times by developing SMI ("Stress Management International"). She had written about it in the African-American press, held up as a role model and, at thirty, pursued by the rich and handsome.

She slowly sat up on the side of the bed, her body aching

slightly from her sixth Capoeira Angola Session.

"Stay down, Valonga, don' get up! Stay down! Make all movements to the floor, don't stand up!" Her thighs twitched as she stood and walked to the window; Bahia, Bahia, Bahia. Capoeira Angola. Candomblé, Africanness in another setting. She stood in the open window, straddle-legged, her arms folded across her breasts, staring down at the cobblestoned streets. The scene was almost familiar by now. Something the Mexicans and Spaniards would call a plaza, cobblestoned streets trickling off from the plaza, exotic calls and responses echoing, distinct smells drifting through her nostrils; garlic, shrimp, palm oil, Bahia seemed to be singing a special song to her.

Welcome Valonga, we are pleased to see you, finally. Welcome, Valonga, is the music lovely to you? Welcome, Valonga, why did it take you so long to return to us? Welcome...

The man's direct look didn't startle her, it wasn't a malevolent look, and she didn't feel as though she were being looked at in a "dirty" way. He was standing in his window, directly across the plaza from her, trying to enjoy the midnight breezes, alert to feelings.

He, too, was naked from the waist up, dark chocolate, gleaming. They took note of each other as though they were scientists. Dark chocolate, muscular male. Nut brown skinned female, smooth. Bold black slitted eyes; sloe eyes, lush printed lips, sensualists. Valonga heard the shadow of a woman's voice speak the man's name before he smiled in her direction, offered a slight bow and ceremoniously closed and serrated wooden windows behind him.

Valonga remained in place, undisturbed by the disappearance of the man in the window across the plaza. There always seems to be a man staring at me from somewhere, in the distance. She looked up at the moon, filled with crinkles of extraterrestrial laughter. Yes, there always seems to be a man staring at me from somewhere. There was a man staring at me from across the inner courtyard in Spain, at the Plaza Matute. His name was Machete and he was a matador, a killer of bulls. His come on was direct, killing. "I am the famous Matador Machete, I have seen you staring at me..."

"I've only seen you once, last Thursday, to be exact, and I wasn't staring at you..."

"I want to give you a ticket to see me fight next Sunday, it will be here in Madrid, you will come?"

"It's one of the reasons why I came to Spain, to experience the corrida."

"How to do this, experience the corrida?"

"I can have the experience by suffering through what the matador goes through."

"You can do this?"

"I can try."

The Candomblé sounds were rising and falling, the rhythms swaying against her. The rhythms created a restless energy in her, made her feel the urge to prowl. She calmly hooked a bra on, pulled a t-shirt on and decided to go for a walk.

"I cannot believe that someone who has not gone into the bullring can experience what the matador may feel."

"Machete" was a Gypsy from the hills of Alicante, filled with the couth and culture of his people.

"Allow me to make a believer of you, take me into the bullring with you."

Valonga Prince, Stress Management Consultant, Inc., President, understood the psychic risks involved.

"Hah, but you might become gored by the bull."

"It is also possible that I might be hit by a Norwegian cab driver. Comprende?"

Valonga strolled the hilly, crooked streets of her section of Bahian territory, understanding the stares of the men who stared at her lush Choctaw-African-French behind; she understood that. It felt good to her, to be physically appreciated, as a woman with a gorgeous shape. She felt the urge to scream out—"hey, I'm fine, can you dig it? and I got brains too!"

But there was no need to do it, there were three large, African-American brothers trailing her, offering a degree of fear and an element of rape. She felt the faint surge of an uncontrollable panic as she turned a corner and made two simultaneous realizations. Number one, the street was unlit and number two the three men were walking beside her.

She decided to go down fighting. She placed her back to the wall and turned to face them with a mean look.

"What do you want...?"

They smiled. The shorter of the three spoke. "We Capoeiristas with you, Capoeira Angola."

She shared their smiles. Of course, Henrique, Nelson and Curio, her classmates at the Academia Capoeira Angola.

"Yes, of course, I didn't recognize you guys for a minute."

They exchanged rapid-soft Bahian Portuguese for a minute before Curio, the English speaker, translated.

"You was scarred shitless, huh?"

"One could say that. Say, where could a lady go for a nice cold beer?"

"Come, we take."

She stared over the contrabarrara at the huge bull prancing across the bullring, Machete's third and last bull of the afternoon.

The bull was what the Spanish called an "authentic cathedral," a five-year-old from the finca of Don Juan Belmonte Garcia of Seville.

15

Valonga felt disgusted. In a mano a mano, fighting three bulls each, Machete had demonstrated all of the bullfighter's worst traits with his two previous bulls.

He had played the first bull so far away from him the crowd whistled like a forest of birds. The second bull, a superior animal, was the catalyst for an attack of cowardice that most of the afición had never seen before. Machete had dived behind the buladero like one of his helpers, he had retreated disgracefully before the bull's honest, straight ahead charge; he had earned the cynical, sarcastic comments from every section of the arena.

"Have you earned too much money, Matador?!"

"Have you no shame, to call yourself a bullfighter?!"

"Use your pistol, man, shoot it before you dishonor the woman who had ya."

"Machete, you bum!!"

Valonga felt the irresistible urge to leave her choice seat and forget about the matador called "Machete." If only I had known what a cheat this guy is. How could the bullfight books glorify this man? Were the pictures faked?

Valonga's urge to leave was canceled by an ambiguous feeling. I'm his guest, how can I leave? She was beginning to understand the meaning of nobility in an animal, watching the bull called "Brujo."

"Brujo" was taken to the horses, received two pics, despite the fact that he clearly demonstrated the ability to absorb more punishment. Valonga stared at Machete's expression; his eyes were gleaming and the solemn look he had held in place for the previous two bulls had disappeared

He waved the bandilleros in his cuadrilla back and took the sticks himself. The afición whistled, some simply frowned . . .

Machete never placed the sticks, why was he doing it now?

The first pair of banderillas stunned them into silence, the second pair, placed as "Machete" faked to his left and neatly dropped them into the bulls hump as he rumbled past, caused the aficion to erupt with "ole's" and applause. The third pair of sticks, broken in half on the edge of the barrera, and placed as cleanly as two pins in a cushion, pulled effervescent applause from the audience.

Valonga settled back into her seat. Was this guy some kind of magician or what? He had suddenly taken them from his degraded position as a dishonorable matador, to another level.

The crude twisting and turning that he had done with bulls number one and two were gone, the awkward motions. He was into a faena that the aficion would talk about for years.

She telescoped the scene, trying to figure out some things. The first bull had been as large, the second, as muscular, both of them filled with courage and speed. She didn't know the names for all the movements that "Machete" was performing with this bull called "Brujo," but she clearly understood that each movement hinted at death.

He used the muleta as though it were a garden gate gently swinging it open inches in front of "Brujo's" huge horns. Left handled naturales. He performed a farolados with the left and right hands, the bull's left and right horns barely missing his eye and skull by inches. "Machete" was giving the bull a fair fight, he was not avoiding the possibility of being killed, or injured. He was giving the bull a fair fight.

He even stopped the whole thing to kiss the bull on the testuz, the forehead, a daring alarde that turned the arena into a screaming madhouse. "Machete" strolled away from the bull's horns, a pleasant expression on his face, an unexpressible arrogance glowing from his movement. Sundunga.

Valonga folded her arms, amazed at the change of moods.

A few minutes ago he was the asshole of the country, now

17

he's the toast of the world. He lined the bull up by slowly moving his muleta from left to right, he profiled a second later and plunged the sword deeply into the area between the bull's shoulder blades.

She was on the verge of screaming for a second, bewildered by the blurred configuration of man, cape, sword and bull. When the pattern cleared itself, the bull had charged the cape in the man's left hand, deflected away from the man's body, as "Machete" plunged the sword in with the right hand. "Machete" had crossed over perfectly. He stood in front of the bull, his arms spread as though he were receiving an offering. The crowd in the arena, screaming and clapping their hands, were obviously far away from his consciousness. "Machete" caught her eye and exchanged thoughts with her as the bull hemorrhaged and keeled over stiff legged, dead by unaware of it.

This is it, "Machete" seemed to be saying with his eyes. This is it, him or me. I won, this time.

The same crowd that whistled earlier, carried "Machete" around the arena on their shoulders, shouting his name and praising him.

The next day she rode beside him on his bull ranch, trying to absorb the feelings of a 150 pound man who had walked into an arena with three animals weighing a half ton each, armed with a piece of cloth, and survived.

"What is the feeling?"

"Yes, what is the feeling? What was the feeling for you yesterday with the first two bulls?"

"Machete" stared at a herd of his prize bulls in a distant pasture, the bill of his cap placing his face in shadows.

"I felt the horns of each of them in my body and I was completely terrified. You must be gored by the bulls to understand what a fear this is. I have been gored many times. They thought I was finished after I was gored in my left buttock. If the horn had been closer it would have gone into my rectum."

Valonga involuntarily made a distasteful expression. "Machete" laughed, swaying with the rhythm of the slow walking horses. "I understand, Valonga, I truly understand, it is an ugly thing to think about."

"So why do you do it if things like that might happen?"

He glanced at her from the corner of his eye, a sneer on his mouth. "You have never been hungry in your life, I can tell. You have no idea what it means to go to bed hungry, night after night, for years. You reach the point of not caring how you get a plate of food, a piece of bread, a soft place to sleep. Some become pickpockets, prostitutes, businessmen, flunkies, emotional suicides, actors...

Some of the more spiritually inclined become bullfighters or priests."

She had heard the connection made before. "What's spirituality got to do with fighting a bull?"

He reigned up and dismounted, motioning for her to do the same. "Come, let us walk for a bit, there is a cool stream just beyond those rocks, in that groove of trees."

They strolled toward the trees, the hot, African sun beaming down on them, summertime in Seville, Moorish Spain.

"Machete" was quiet until they entered the shade of the trees, sat on some rocks near the narrow stream.

"The spiritual part is not always there. It wasn't there for me with the first two bulls yesterday. I felt nothing but fear, and the fear prevented me from behaving in a sacred manner. But you must admit, it was there for "Brujo."

She nodded in agreement.

"No one can explain why it is there, or why it is *not* there. There are times when I feel it will be there and it is not and I am surprised. And at other times, when it shouldn't be there, it is. It happened last year in Valencia, for example. I was high and the bulls were treacherous. I had the feeling that both of my bulls had been fought before. It seemed that they clearly understood the difference between the man and the muleta, but they couldn't touch me. I was, how do you say, invincible. I could do anything."

Valonga suddenly froze as four bulls casually strolled up to the water, about ten yards downstream. They looked like prehistoric monsters.

"Keep your voice low, they may not notice us. The have their own conversations." They stared at the bulls, measuring the size of their horns, the huge hump of muscle above the shoulders, the heavy sleek bodies. The bulls glanced up at them in a nearsighted way a couple of times, and finally, after long minutes of drinking, they ambled away, disappearing into the trees.

"I never realized how wild they are."

"Yes, you see now that we are the tame ones and they are the wild, free ones."

They took off their boots and dangled their feet in the stream.

"Valonga, you understand now that we are priests, we are the men who take the chances in the arena, who make the sacrifices so that certain forces in our deeper feelings will be eased by the blood. We are priests."

She looked wan at the rocks in the stream. "Can anyone become a priest?"

"Maybe yes, maybe no. The bulls determine that, they pick and choose."

They put their boots back on and started back to the grand ranch home that overlooked his thousand acres.

"Will I have a chance to experience this screening out process?"

"We will be fighting calves this afternoon, after the

siesta."

Flamenco started the afternoon. Valonga slid off of her siesta bed and stared at "Machete" sprawled in a nearby chair.

"It would be better if I took my siesta in your room, it will make people think better of me, that I am macho. Sometimes people make up stories, you know what I mean?"

"What will they think of me?"

"You are outside our culture, it doesn't matter. You are a Black American woman, you can do, or people think that you can do everything. You could pull up your dress and shit in the streets and people would applaud you. This is Southern Spain, this is where we civilized the Europeans."

"But you're a Spaniard, a European."

"No, Valonga, I am a Gypsy . . . being a Gypsy in Spain is like what it was like to be a Black in America.

We are African from Egypt, many, many centuries ago, and many of them hate us because of our history, like your people in America. Some of them love us, because of our history. But they cannot get rid of us. You know, for some people, the image of Spain is the Gypsy soul."

Everything was cool so long as "Machete" could pretend that he was fucking Valonga, just for the sake of appearances. Bullfighting, etiquette demanded it. Spain demanded it.

She shook him awake from his hap on the sofa in her room.

"It is time?" he asked, his eyes opening to focus on a faraway point.

"It is time," she answered him solemnly, going with the moment.

He left her room gently closing the door behind.

"See you in the arena."

Chapter 2

Matador Manuel Arruza, "Machete," was allowing her the chance to cape a couple fighting female bulls; their horns were short but they turned quickly and were quite aggressive. They were going to be pic'ed, to determine whether or not they had the traits that a bull ranch breeder wanted to continue in his herd, or emphasize, or whatever.

And the whole thing was going to be done as though it was a real bullfight, complete with a fake banderilla section. "Machete" loved the idea of the staging of a bullfight on his finca. He was delighted to participate. She was given the opportunity to perform each of the jobs that led to the kill.

She started off, naturally, as one of the picadores. That really felt strange, to sit astride a horse with something that looked and felt like a sharpened tent pole, waiting for these small, aggressive mothers of bulls-to-be, to charge. "Remember, hit her in the center where the muscle is, not too far back. Relax.''

Valonga sat the horse well, she had learned how to ride when her father was alive. "Val, everybody should know how to ride a horse, they can teach us a lot." Her father, she remembered, was a very complicated man. Had been.

The bull trotting in toward her quilted-padded horse startled her. The females, at whatever age they took this test, were not as small as she had been led to believe.

"Machete" himself took the bull away from the pics with gracefully ambulating chicuelinas.

Valonga stared at the man weaving himself in and out of a cape, within and out of the bull's vision, tailoring his movements to fit the bull's clear, clean charge.

"This one," he indicated to a ranch foreman with one hand while he befuddled the poor animal with an old-fashioned serpentine rebolera. Next, they gave Valonga wooden stakes, weighing as much as banderillas, and said, "pretend that you are placing the sticks. Do it, get the feeling of it. But be careful, she knows we can cause her pain now, and she is much more cautious now than she was at the beginning. Bulls learn very quickly, especially the smart mothers."

Valonga was told to "place" one pair of banderillas al quiebro. She was to stand in place, let the bull begin her charge, lean slightly to the left or right, and as the bull rumbled past, punch the sticks into the hump on her back. It seemed as though the stands were suddenly packed with people. Everything was right there for everybody to see.

The bull took forever to charge her and when she did, she wheeled and charged as though she had been struck by an electric volt.

Valonga had a second to compose herself, to remember to keep her feet together, left her arms with the blunt banderillas and slowly attract the charging bull's attention by leaning to the left or right.

24

She chose to fake to the left. The bull went for the fake three-fourths of the way before realizing that she had been faked out. She stopped in the middle of her charge and tossed her head, braced by miniature horns, causing Valonga to jump back in self-defense.

"Berry good, Valonga! Berry good, Valonga!" "Machete" shouted over the berrera.

She walked stiff-legged out of the bull's field of vision, as a peon lured the animals attention to another area of the arena.

"Now, for the faena," "Machete" spoke quietly to hear as he gave her the muleta and the wooden sword that was sometimes used as a support for the muleta. "Valonga, you must remember that she runs fast, so you must speed up your cape work. You understand?"

She numbly nodded and moved back into the center of the arena. She had to remind herself that this arena was only an attachment of the estate, it wasn't the Plaza Madrid, or the Plaza Mexico, or any of the great bullrings in the world. It could've been any of the great bullrings in the world so far as she was concerned. The bull, "Melina," evidently shared her opinion. She charged as though her hooves were glued to rails. Valonga decided to open her faena with as many slow passes as she could manage.

"Melina," catching the lure and following it like a house cat moving toward a bowl of fresh milk, surprised her.

The pase de la muerte led her into doing a trio of naturales with the left and right hand. "Melina" was attentive and followed the lure eagerly. The muleta and fake sword was dragged from her hand at the completion of the third natural.

"Machete," showing great concern, dashed from behind the buladero to distract the bull as she raced around the ring, Valonga's muleta snagged on her right horn. One of his peons snatched the muleta from the bull's horn. "Machete," lured the furiously charging animal into his capote for a few media verónicas.

Valonga stood over to one side, excited by the beauty of "Machete's" clever use of the large cape. After a couple more passes, he finished up by literally hypnotizing the bull into a trance, with a serpentine motion of the capote. He strolled away, looking as though he were taking a walk on one of the boulevards.

"Now, Valonga, the moment of truth," he whispered to her. He handed her a short, slender knife.

"What do I do with this?"

"I want you to profile, just as I've taught you to do, and cross the bull as you plunge this into the bull's hump. She won't be hurt very much and we can shoot her full of antibiotics to heal her. Are you ready?"

Valonga nodded, beginning to feel as though she were in a strange dream. She was going to kill a bull, symbolically.

"Melina" trotted from one side of the arena to another, pausing to stare at different objects. She was obviously angry, as angry as a female bull can feel.

Valonga walked quickly to the center of the area and made a roundabout gesture, indicating that the "kill" she was about to make was for all the people in the arena.

The aficion applauded, "Melina" charged. Valonga whirled her muleta with a movement that deflected the bull's aim.

"Ole!" "Machete" shouted from beyond the barrera.

Valonga took heart from the encouragement and tried two more passes. "Maelina" stood stock still for a few moments after the last pass.

Now, now, Valonga whispered to herself, the moment of truth.

She profiled and moved toward "Melina" as "Melina" charged her. Valonga felt a sharp jab in her right thigh and

26

suddenly saw stars and the world twirling around inside her head.

She came back to her senses sprawled on a deck chair on the veranda of the finca. "Machete" was bending over her, smiling, a servant stood nearby.

"Valonga, are you O.K.?"

She nodded yes, yes, I'm O.K..

"Did I, did I make the kill?"

"Machete" smiled and held up an ancient, dried up ear from another bull that he had killed years before. They looked at the ear and burst into rib tickling, contagious laughter. She didn't realize she had been gored slightly in the upper right thigh until the laughter broke one of her stitches.

"Oh my God!"

"Don't worry, it is only a slight wound, it will heal berry quickly."

"Machete" used her wound as an excuse to keep her as a guest for an extra week. "Don't you see, Valonga, it will look bad if you leave now, people will think badly of our relationship."

She decided to humor the situation by remaining on the ranch. The wound required twelve stitches and was painful healing, itchy. "Machete" gave her cocoa butter to help the healing process.

"Use this three times a day and you will hardly have a scar when the wound heals."

"Machete" made no further efforts to seduce her, but still made very effort to maintain his Gypsy-Casanova image by having long conversations in her bedroom late at night, mostly about the corrida, fueled by glasses of Jerez de la Frontera.

"I know that there are many who would disagree with this, but I think the matador is one of the great coquettes of the world. He is, how you say, a bery great flirt."

"I'm not sure I understand."

"Let me try to make clear. The bull is a true symbol of macho, you understand?"

"Without a doubt."

"The man, any man, no matter how macho he is, can never be as much macho as the bull. In many ways, the man is really a woman in disguise."

Valonga readjusted her wounded leg on the ottoman and sat up a little straighter.

"A woman in disguise?"

"Yes, I believe. Here we have this man who is not like other men. We are slim."

"Machete" stood and twirled around in an unselfconscious way, as though showing off a movement, rather than himself.

"We are hairless, no one has ever seen a real bullfighter with a beard. We wear tightly fitted clothes with sequins and bright colors, we flirt with the bull. We wave red capes in front of him, to trick him into doing what we want him to do. Isn't that what women do, with their perfumes, pretty clothes, and graceful movements?"

Valonga thought about it for a few moments and gave a qualified nod—yes—to his question.

"And finally, after we have confused him into a kind of trance, we stick it in and he dies."

"But isn't that a reversal of the man-woman thing?"

"Not really, because, you see, even if the man kills the bull he also dies, because the bull is the man and the man is also the bull."

Many of the midnight conversations ended on a slightly confused note, but there were several clear points made.

"Make no doubt about it, Valonga, we are priests, making a sacrifice for the benefit of the aficion. We are shedding blood, sometimes ours, always the bulls, to purge the souls of all of those who come to our events, no matter whether

28

they sit in the shade or the sun.

"As a Gypsy, I can say to you that I understand the nature of the corrida better than the payos. We Gypsies are the soul of Spain and they know it. In many ways we are like the Black people of your country."

"Machete" was right about the effect of the coca butter; she had used it religiously for a few months and the gash in her thigh had healed with barely a trace.

"Machete" had been emotionally disturbed when she announced that it was time for her to leave.

"But, Valonga, there is so much more to talk about. The season is starting in two weeks, you will have the opportunity to see me fight the bulls all over Spain."

"Yes, I know, "Machete," I know, but I must go. I have my own season to attend to."

She felt a slight twinge in her upper right thigh, where the cow had torn a gash.

Henrique, Nelson and Curio smothered her with attention.

"Valonga, you want another Brahma?"

She smiled and nodded no, she was still sipping a half-full bottle. They sprawled around a table in a bar that resembled an open storefront. Men, women, children moved in and out; groups of men, clustered at one table discussing the relative merits of various soccer players, a pair of serious lovers huddled in a far corner, whispering into each other's ears.

She liked the openness of the bars, the lack of a Puritanical sense of shame that closed North American saloons up behind thick doors and neon signs. People here wanted to drink beer, cachacfa, have a good time without guilt.

"People come to Brazil to study Capoeira Regional, you come for Capoeira Angola. Why?"

Curio, the translator, was kept busy asking the questions that his two non-English speaking friends wanted to have

29

answered.

"Because Capoeira Angola is deeper, more African."

She was grateful, for once, that the translation process gave her time to really think about what she wanted to say and to say it as briefly and clearly as possible.

"Valonga, Henrique wants to know what you think of Mestre Juizo?"

She slowly turned her beer bottle around in the wet circle on the table. "What do I think of him?"

"I am a master of Capoeira Angola. Pay attenshun!"

She did a quickie play back of her past two weeks in O Grupo Capoeira Angola Bahia.

Mestre Juizo was a master, there was no doubt about that. It was apparent from the strange gleam in his eyes and the radar feel he had for being in the right place at the right time.

She had taken classes in West African dance, been a serious jogger at one point, never allowed herself to get out of condition, and none of it seemed to matter with Capoeira Angola.

The deceptively simple movements, the calmly moving cartwheels, and the monkey-like ginga were strenuous enough to make her feel totally exhausted after fifteen minutes.

"I think Mestro Juizo is a great psychologist."

Curio translated her answer and the three men sipped their beers and nodded in agreement.

"Pay attenshun!"

The Mestre had never questioned her about why she wanted to study Capoeira Angola, he seemed to know why. It was though this martial art that he knew, that he taught, dealt more with the mind than with any movement of the body.

"Pay attenshun!"

The class started promptly at 7 p.m. and almost had an

aimless quality to it. Fifteen minutes were devoted to complex but simple movements.

"Negativa, rastiera. This way!" And he would demonstrate. He was impatient, but always seemed to have the time to show the struggling student the correct way to make a movement.

She studied him as he studied them. He had the ability, it seemed, to know exactly what thirty people were doing and whether or not they were doing it correctly.

"This is Meia Lua. Pay attenshun!"

The movements of Capoeira Angola, fortified by its music, were designed to fit the natural motions of the body, the ability to attack built into each movement.

She was frequently confused by the seemingly ambivalent nature of this African-Brazilian martial art; the way it flowed from innocence to sophistication, from gentleness to violent eruptions.

"Think what you're doing!"

She felt comfortable in the art, driven to make movements she'd never thought about making.

"Don't kick too high!"

The Mestre pushed, pulled at their psyches, coerced them into understanding the nature of his art.

"Capoeira Angola is what you eat, it is how you sleep, what you dream, it is life."

"Machete" had said that, in a slightly different way.

"Remember, Valonga, the bull represents life and the horns can pierce you at any time."

Strangely, she felt, no one had questioned her reasons for wanting to study Capoeira Angola up 'til now. She smiled at her three companions. They instantly returned her smile.

"Why Capoeira Angola, Valonga?"

"You already asked me that."

"No, I didn't, Nelson asked."

31

Curio added the gleam of his eyes to his smile.

"Why?"

She felt uncertain if he would understand that she knew the difference between Capoeira Regional and Capoeira Angola.

"Well, I explained earlier that I feel that Capoeira Angola is deeper, more African."

She paused for him to translate. The couple in the corner were slowly walking out, the man's left arm around the woman's waist. The men discussing the merits of various soccer player's had become a bit more lively. She frequently heard the names Pelé and Garrinche mentioned.

"Explain more, please."

She signaled for another round of beers.

"This one is on me. Well, I'm sure you guys must know, better than I do, that Capoeira Angola came about many years before Capoeira Regional, maybe hundreds, even thousands of years before."

Curio translated, using his hands to explain her time reference.

"And that's what I wanted to get into, I wanted to get involved with the root of the matter, not the branches, I mean, if you knew that it was possible to have the goose who laid golden eggs, why settle for the silver eggs?"

They raised their bottles of beer in a toast—salute to her. She felt moved by the gesture.

Chapter 3

"NO! NO! NO! No, Valonga! You must keep the fingers together, the sound must be solid, complete, O.K.?! Now, once again, let's play the rhythm together."

She studied his hands as they sat opposite each other and stroked the rhythm. Bright, tropical sun gleamed beyond the open door, chickens pecked around on the front porch.

His hands are more like paws than hands, like fleshy drumsticks.

"Now you," he said suddenly.

He cast a sly smile in her direction. Senor Bá has caught you daydreaming again, huh?

She floundered off into what she thought he had played. She sounded confused, dazed.

"No, thass not it," he announced quietly and sat back to wait for her to figure out what she had done wrong.

He was Armando Bá, the coldest conga, Bata, and Bongo

man to ever emigrate to the states, play with all the best people and leave them, in his prime, to return to his home village in the hills of eastern Cuba.

Cuba was Bá, Bá was Cuba. Some people saw him as a modern Orisha, as blasphemous as that may sound to others, a drum deity.

There were nights in nightclubs across the world where Armando had appeared, sometimes with jaded white men, filled with creative juices, doing things with his hands on the conga that made people scream. Scream out loud, open, full, scream!!

He healed with his playing. Malevolent spirits were ripped from their moorings and floated downstream.

Love poured from the rafters. Listening to the hard, velvet touch of his hands, he was Master Bá, the soul of Afro-Cuban music in Cuba.

She nudged him to wake him up, to let him know she had figured out what she had done wrong.

"Some things I only tell you once, Valonga, only wan time. You not understand, your problem, O.K.?"

They were becoming the darlings of his village. The people felt that Master Bá had been rewarded in his old age with a beautiful young African-American woman, and they liked that. They couldn't figure the drum angle out. What was she really there for? Her goal was to do six months of Bá, she had done her research; Bá was the master of one of the most complicated systems of music in the world, Afro-Cuban music, and she wanted to experience that.

Bá understood her. He understood everything, you could tell that from the way he looked at you, that was the way one who had mastered something could look at you.

The lessons were intense, filled with logic and tension.

"No, No, Valonga, your ritmo cannot be casual, it mus' always be strong and right where it is supposed to be, you

34

must know your place.''

She hated the logic of it. Why couldn't they just simply play. Just enjoy the sound of the drums?

"No, Valonga, the drums are sacred, not to enjoy only, but to speak for the Orisha, to bring elements into play, to open doors. The drum is berry powerful instrument.

"They always want to take the drum away from us. You know? Everywhere we have the drum they say 'queek! Take his drum! Take his drum.'''

The non-African don't know this language, they fear it, so they forbid it.''

Valonga was frequently freaked out by the precision of Bá's language. There were times when it seemed almost childlike, but precise and clean.

He was self-educated, meaning he had been one of the last members of his generation to carry water into the sugar cane fields for $1.00 a day.

"Si, one dollar a day.''

A political to the bone, he could say that with profound disgust.

They had classes four times weekly, and each class was a serious emotional event for both of them.

She had fallen in love with him at their first meeting, a serious, daughterly love.

"Why you want the drum?''

"Because it is an unexplored part of my psyche, and I want to know it, to map it out, know as much as I can about it.

She was never fully certain that her answer was the "right" one, but he took her on as a student anyway.

"Valonga, the sound of the drum is sweet, but to learn it is not sweet.''

"I'm willing to try.''

The village of Bocagrande watched them with acute interest, monitored the success, or failure of each lesson with

35

smiles of pleasure, and/or sympathetic frowns.

Children stood in the open doorway of Bá's house to watch her stumble through her lessons, their dark eyes bright and serious. On those days when she successfully negotiated her way through some simple rhythm, they smiled shyly at her.

At other times she was embarrassed by not being able to count properly.

"I want you to count to four; won, two, three, fou... You unnerstand? Won *and* two *and*..."

After she had struggled thru the process several times, he might call to one of the children in the door.

"Jose!" Or, "Maria!"

He would tell them the name of the rhythm and they would play it, hesitantly, but they would play it.

She left his home to wander thru the streets of Bocagrande, dazed by the hundreds of things she had to know in order to play one single, simple rhythm well.

"The drum is berry sensitive, Valonga, he can tell if you are not sure of yourself, or if you are lying about your place in the rhythm. You unnerstand?"

She sprawled across her bed in the Casa Castro, sipping the local sweet rum and scribbling notes in her notebook.

"Master Bá is like masters everywhere, he knows what he knows as well as anyone can know it and that makes him a master."

Bocagrande was intensely hospitable to her, she literally had to stay out of sight in order to avoid invitations to come and eat, attend the baptism of a baby, be a part of the community.

She was Armando Bá's student and that gave her instant entree.

"You are freen of Senor Bá, you are my freen."

The village was almost a backward look at another time; had it not been for electric lights and running water, she could easily have been into another age.

The people were basically African, the Indian and European strands gently woven into the slanted eyes, the unusually straight hair of some of the people. Bá was one of the patriarchs of the village.

"My great grandfather and his wife were the people who first make this place. You unnerstand?"

It was one of those days when the sun seemed hotter than usual, the humidity higher, the lesson of the day had left her feeling drained and sticky, but satisfied.

"Not so bad as last time, Valonga. Les have a ron y coke."

Sitting on the shady porch of his comfortable house, sipping an after-the-lesson rum and coke, quietly watching an ancient Cuban stroll past, he talked about life, the drum, the past, the future.

"Yes, Castro deed a lot for Cuba. Before Castro like the Africans in Alabama before King, were treated like dirt. My granfather used to tell me stories about how badly we were treated. We were close to being slaves. You dig?"

The man was full of twists and slips. His language, for example, would sometimes slip from NBC English up to Chicago Southside jazz accented dialect of Post Bop. She was forced to remember that Bá had lived in the "States" for years and played with some of the hippest musicians in the world.

"When deed I start to play the drum?"

"No. Why?"

"It was there, someone had to play them."

She was never certain that he wasn't putting her on. Sometimes he wasn't.

"I was not a drummer in the beginning, I was a dancer."

She could see it. Despite the slight black beans and rice paunch, he was still able to indicate, with superbly subtle movements of his body, how a particular rhythm should go.

37

"Wha' happen? I was hangin' out with Mongito, Pablo, Carlos, Peraza, Francisco, Chaco, and dudes like that, all drummers. They say to me: "Eh, Armando, play this part."

"So wha' happen? I play. The Jesus Maria district was where it was happenin' in those days, in La Habana."

He startled her by scooting out of his easy chair to do a few mambo steps that looked like oil sliding back 'n forth on water. He stopped as suddenly as he had started and slipped back into his chair, a little out of breath from the exertion.

"I was the best, you unnerstand? I was the best. My favorite partner was La Lupe."

He paused for a meditative sip on his ron y coke.

"La Lupe *was* Afro-Cuban rhythm. Som'times, when she was at her berry best, people would move over to the side of the dance floor to watch us dance, en La Habana, you unnerstand?"

Valonga, buzzed on the ron, the humidity and the atmosphere that enveloped her, nodded slowly, yes, I unnerstand.

"There are people who say—yes, they say that. There are people who say that I became who I am because I had my hands washed by Iyalosha Songobumni."

She stared stupidly at him for a few moments, close to being drunk, before she was able to form the question.

"Your hands washed?"

"Yes, washed," he answered, without affirming or denying the validity of the question. A moment later he slid out of his chair, disappeared inside the house, and returned with a thick scrapbook.

"Here, look."

He let her flip thru several pages without comment. Pictures of men with Bata drums on their thighs, pictures of events from the past, history.

"I cannot explain who these people are to you because they would not mean more if I explain. You unnerstand?"

She nodded, understanding. The air was suddenly cool, filled with the hint of rain.

"Feels like rain."

"No, just the magic of these pictures...these pictures represent when I was being taken into the world of the drums. You unnerstand, Valonga?"

She nodded, not fully understanding if she understood or not. One thing was absolutely certain, she was being made aware of people, places, and events that she would not have known about.

"This man, Macucho, sang like chocolate. It is exactly as I am saying it, like chocolate."

She fell into his food adjectives, understanding, for the first time.

"La Lupe was the aroma of the Cuban cigar. She addicted many of us to the sound of her voice."

Valonga stared at the photograph of a Black queen with heavy buttered buns, an effervescently wide mouth and a look in her eyes that offered any kind of satisfaction a man needed. She recalled a page of her research.

"Armando, was La Lupe a prostitute?"

"La Lupe was an artist," he answered, closing off any further discussion.

Bá was Cuba, Oriente, and Oriente was Bá.

They were interrupted during the course of every class by someone wanting to know something that only Bá could know.

"We cannot find the rhythm for this event, it predates the date that we have been given."

"What is the event, please?"

"It is for when a man has had a child by a woman and, years later, decides to adopt that child, and a particular

39

rhythm is played.''

"AAAAhhhh, Somoloruko; that is the rhythm.''

He knew rhythms and messages that he had learned when he was five years old, lessons 65 years old. Valonga was awed by his knowledge.

"But Valonga, this is the way it is fer us, I am a master of the drum.''

It would've sounded like an arrogant statement if anyone else had made it, but coming from Armando Bá, it seemed the proper statement to make.

"When I realized what a burden I had placed on myself, I felt berry sick.''

Armando Bá humble? It was unbelievable.

"Ahh yes, Valonga, it is true. I was berry much frightened by this responsibility.''

The days of drumming, of trying to drum, of trying to find out what secrets the drums would reveal to her, of trying to understand the healing power of the drums, caused her many sleepless nights. She began to relate Bá.

Nelson, Henrique and Curio were very close to being drunk, it was difficult to identify the state of their being because they were Angolieres.

They sidestepped, Samba-motioned through the streets of her neighborhood, earnestly searching for the best way to say something about how they felt.

Curio, the translator, surrendered his duty to Nelson, at one point, forcing him to understand English, a language he felt was reserved for old school teachers and mongrel dogs.

"It's such a growlly langish.''

They shared a laugh. I guess English *would* sound like a bunch of dogs growling, compared to the nasal music of Bhaian Portuguese.

It was getting close to midnight and the cobblestoned streets were almost deserted. The clear sounds of people chanting, a bell being stroked and drums being played floated on the humid air.

"That's Candomblé, isn't it?"

The question was clear, even to the non-English speakers. They nodded.

"Is it far away?"

Curio looked her in the eye, solemnly.

"No, not too far."

"Can we go there?" she asked impulsively.

He translated the question and engaged in a rapid fire dialogue with his friends.

"Yes, we can go there, I know people of this terriero, but Henrique and Nelson say they cannot go, have other things to do, getting up early tomorrow."

They shook hands and exchanged kisses on both cheeks with her.

"Ciao, Valonga."

"Ciao, Henrique."

"Adeus, Valonga."

"Adeus, Nelson."

She watched them walk away, proud young African men, filled with the knowledge of Capoeira Angola, that gave them an air of confidence.

"Come, it is this way."

They strolled through the dimly lit, cobblestoned street. Bahia. She felt the history of the place when she said the word silently.

Bahia, an Africa transported to the New World, rich with customs, art, emotions, Capoeira Angola de Bahia.

"Curio, how long have you studied with Mestre Juizo?"

"Six years."

"Six years, why so long?"

She could read the puzzled expression on his face in the

dim light/shadow of the streets.

"Not so long, Capoeira Angola is muito complexed."

"Yes, it is complex."

She suddenly felt like one of those fast food Americans, who thought that anything that took longer than a year was too long.

Here I am, after all two weeks, asking this dude why he's been studying for six years.

"Mestre Juizo is a good teacher, no?"

"Yes, Mestre Juizo is a very good teacher."

She quickly reviewed her "Mestre Juizo tape" again. The man could've been an Amazonian Indian if his hair weren't so nappy. Short, about 5'8" or so, but loose jointed.

She was really surprised to learn that he was forty-three years old, she had thought he was in his late twenties.

"Capoeira Angola is good for me, it keeps me young."

He had a clear sense of humor, sometimes made fun of his English—"I speak English better every time I have to"—loved for children to come to the roda, love beautiful women—"you are lovely, Valonga, you know?" But when the class started he was merciless.

"Pay attenshun!"

He made them repeat simple movements over and over.

"Valonga, no, not like that, like this. Do the movement exactly like I show you. EXACTLY!"

After two weeks she had been privileged to see the Mestre play twice. She wasn't certain of what she had been exposed to, the first time.

She was more attentive the second time, and even more bewildered. He seemed to take all of the simple movements he was teaching and fused them into a complex stream of flowing motions.

His ginga seemed to be the careless behavior of a drunk, but each motion, when she analyzed it, was beautifully choreographed. The drunken ginga would suddenly become an explosive attack, a tiger springing from knee-high grass.

He never seemed to attack any point above the waist, and when he did attack, with heel, toe, knee, side of the head, edge of hand, or a devastatingly disarming smile, he was always on the target.

"We are almost there, just up this alley."

The chanting and drumming didn't seem any louder than it had sounded from a distance, now that they were in the outer courtyard of the terriero.

Chapter 4

She was feeling the rhythms better, she could tell because Master Bá didn't find it necessary to correct her as often. Three months of simple exercises, left hand, right hand, left hand right hand...simple rhythms.

"Today, Valonga, we are going to sit in the back under the tree and play a little guaguanco. Okey dokey? First, I'm going to carry the rhythm and you will play the quinto, and then I am going to play the quinto and you will carry the rhythm. Let's go hit it!"

She helped carry his drums out into the backyard, a spacious area filled with several banana trees and other tropical vegetation. It wasn't cutely manicured and gave the appearance of a low-level jungle.

He brought a fifth of rum and half a bottle of coke out, placed them on a nearby table. "We may need this before the session is over."

Children of all ages and sizes immediately put in an appearance, followed by a few curious adults. Anything that happened in and around Amando Bá's house was always "news." He sat across from her and with the first strokes wove a wall of lush rhythm around her. He made it impossible *not* to play. He nodded with his chin for her to come in.

The solid wall of rhythm intimidated her for a few beats. He nodded a little more urgently, and frowned. She came in on time, self-consciously aware of how elementary her quinto ideas were.

"Don't play a lot, better a few things well than lots of stuff."

A few more people arrived, smiling at the sight of the old master and his American student. After five minutes she was coated with a fine film of perspiration and her arms felt like dead weights. A couple of teenagers wandered into the yard, bowed politely to the drummers and began to dance. A couple of the smaller children began to imitate them.

Valonga suddenly felt her arms lighten, and her hands seemed to be fluttering onto the drumhead without any conscious effort on her part.

Bá smiled.

"Whaddaya say, we change. O.K.?"

She was flattered by the applause and didn't know whether to bow, smile or pretend not to hear.

"Smile a little, Valonga, the people are pleased with you."

She could tell from the way he phrased the statement that he was also pleased. They took a little break to sip some rum, while lesser talents filled the gap. The backyard was suddenly filled with the villagers of Bocagrande. They laughed, shook her hand, smiled at her, offered eloquent toasts for her efforts.

"Senor Bá, what did he say?"

"He said that he thought you play very good."

"Is that all?"

"Isn't that enough? You wan' heem to say you play like me?"

Japan, after Cuba felt like a cultural corset. She strolled the streets of Okayama, subconsciously listening for the sound of the conga, the chatter of bongos or the cling clang of the agogo.

"You will think about us, here in Bacagrande, we will be in your mind."

She had made a fine-tuned decision not to delay her motion, once she had reached a certain level, not to delay after she had reached a certain point of development with the drum.

Bá understood.

"Heyyyy, whaddaya tryin' to do? Make yourself feel bad? Shit! (he pronounced it sheet) you came here, you know what I mean: you came to nibble on the edge of the drum with Papa Bá, now you wanna go. Is O.K.? Sure, is O.K.! You didn't come here pretending to be a serious student of the drum."

She flinched involuntarily, accepting his correct assessment of her as a non-serious drummer.

"I mean, c'mon, les git real 'round here. How much of the drum can you really get under your belt in three-four months?"

"You're right, you know that?"

"Yes, you bet yo' durty draws I'm right. But I gotta say this to you. I never had a student with a mind like yours, Valonga, if you wanted to spend the time, you could become a top-flight drummer."

"How long would it take?"

"Four, maybe fibe years..."

She passed a narrow side street and walked back to it. Someone was playing a drum.

She listened closely. No, no koto master here, just someone banging on a pair of Christmas tree bongos. She continued her search. The taxi driver wasn't certain where #369 was. He had simply overcharged her, politely opened the door of his vehicle to let her out and advised her to, "ask people, this Eta district, everybody know koto master."

She had landed in Tokyo two days before and immediately taken a train to Okayama, the home of master Kimio Eta, the blind man who was acknowledged to be one of the greatest koto players in the world.

Children in their neat uniforms of blue and white pointed at her and giggled, "Gaijin! Gaijin!"

She smiled in reply and continued wandering. There were, strangely, enough addresses in English for her to be encouraged. She wasn't feeling particularly discouraged, for some reason.

The town was picturesque, the people provincial but not obnoxious, and she felt that she would be able to find Master Eta. It was in her bones.

She turned the corner and stood there, her lower jaw slack, shocked at the sight of the giant cut out of Colonel Sanders.

"Well, I'll be damned!"

She canceled out her ambivalence and walked through the doors anyway. What the hell! a piece of chicken is a piece of chicken.

The business of the place seemed to suspend itself when she entered. She suddenly felt like a weird kind of celebrity. All eyes turned to stare at her. It was obvious that they didn't serve gaijin often, and probably they had never seen an African-American gaijin before.

Valonga studied the pictures of the pieces of chicken. Such a good idea to show the food. One picture *is* worth a thousand words.

She was forced to the head of the line by a short queue

of fried chicken lovers. She made attempts to decline but they ignored her and bowed her to the front anyway.

The young man behind the counter brightened and self-consciously straightened his cap as she wavered between the six pieces of chicken with coleslaw or the luncheon special with mashed potatoes and gravy.

"I am English," the man behind the counter spoke, jarring her decision to choose the luncheon special.

"Really?"

"Yes, I can help you."

The man's heavy accent and his super sincere manner almost caused her to laugh, but she checked the impulse. Why make enemies on your first day in town?

"Yes, you do speak English quite well and you may be able to help me."

He bowed slightly, indicating his willingness to serve.

She decided impulsively to make a stab in the dark.

"Do you know where Master Kimio Eta lives?"

The superficial grin disappeared from his face as the meaning of her question sank in.

"Ah so, yes, Master Eta, I know."

"Can you tell me how to get to his house?"

She glanced behind her. The "inscrutable" Asian faces were beginning to betray some annoyance at the amount of time she was using to make her order.

"One hour more here, I take you Master Era house."

An hour later Valonga was being led thru the narrow streets of the oldest section of Okayama by Kunzai Ozawa, Colonel Sanders employee and devoted English student.

"I learn English alone."

He tried every phrase he had learned over the course of a two-year period.

"Please, how do you say?"

Valonga was beginning to feel worn out.

"Uhh, Kunzai, are we close to the Master's house?"

"Close, coming close."

She managed to cut off another stream of questions by making the universal gesture for "be quiet."

It was twilight in Okayama and she felt as though she had been transported to a medieval Japan.

They passed curtained bar doors where men sat around low tables drinking sake, laughing, talking loud in guttural voices. The contrast between the ultra-polite people she had been exposed to earlier and these rough types was startling.

Men with cigarette stubs clenched in the corners of their mouths eyed them cynically, made coarse jokes.

"Kunzai, what did that man say?"

"Did not understand, Eta slung."

"Slang, you mean."

"Yes, slang, dif'cult to translate."

The smell of fish, rice, pickled foods, charcoal smoke on the air lured her away from more questions.

She accepted the attention she received, negative or positive. Capoeira Angola had plowed a fatalistic mindset into her head. Some people will like you, some people will not like you, play your own game.

The music drifting over the low bamboo wall mimicked the smell of fish and rice.

Kunzai didn't have to tell her that they were standing in front of Master Eta's house. Kunzai squatted near the wall, motioned for her to join him.

"Koto nice, huh?" he asked her.

Valonga stared at her guide's face. Nice?

It was the most banal word she could ever imagine to use, to describe what they were hearing. Some of the chords could only be called delicious, others, passionately exquisite. For a stretch of five minutes or so they listened to sounds that seemed to be reflections of something beautiful floating on a still pool of water.

Nice?

The music seemed to wander at time, as though it were nomadic, searching for a place no one had ever been exposed to.

Valonga stood slowly. She knew something about the history of the koto and quite a bit about Master Eta, but had never experienced the music live.

Master Kimio Eta, born July 6th, 1937, Okayama, Japan, blind since birth, orphaned at five years old, apprenticed at 7 years old to a barrel maker, beaten like a beast for every mistake he made.

Discovered to have a perfect ear for the Koto, "purchased" from the barrel maker for $25.00 by an aristocratic family, given the best musical education Japan could offer, recorded by a small, but influential Japanese record company (Banzai Productions), unknown to the west, except for esoteric types like Valonga.

Valonga saw Kunzai make a surreptitious study of his watch and suddenly realized that she had taken advantage of the young man's time; "Kunzai, I'm sorry, I know your family must be worried about you by now."

Kunzai Ozawa puffed his chest out with an exaggerated show of machismo.

"No problem. No problem"

Valonga weighed the possibilities impulsively, but carefully.

Damn, how do I handle this?

"Kunzai, I want you to knock on the gate and translate what I say to whoever comes to answer. O.K.?"

What the hell, why not go for the whole avocado?

The sudden light from a lantern being lit behind the wall captured the quizzical expression on Kunzai Ozawa's face.

"Kunzai, do you understand?"

"Hai, yes, I understand."

The plucked notes of the koto seemed to underscore her hesitant knocking, and then they faded out. She knocked again, feeling like the worst example of what Colonel Sanders' chicken and American insolence could give birth to. She was about to knock again, her heart pounding almost as loud as the sound she was making on the bamboo gate.

The face of a tiny Simian appeared as the gate was slowly opened. It took Valonga a few beats to realize that it was the face of a woman. She didn't speak, she didn't seem surprised, she simply waited, her expression neutral.

Valonga took note of the flurry of discordant notes coming from some inner place.

"Kunzai, please tell this lady that my name is Valonga Prince, that I am a great admirer of Master Eta's music and that I would like to meet him."

The woman with the monkey face listened to the translation, again without a change of expression and when it was finished she answered and slowly closed the gate.

Kunzai and Valonga stared at the gate as though they had seen a mirage, the notes of the koto suddenly seemed distant, ethereal.

"Well, what did she say?" Valonga asked impatiently.

Kunzai shook his head from side to side, obviously puzzled.

"She say...ahh..."

Valonga drove on him, determined to get a translation that wasn't watered down by cultural considerations, she didn't want to be told what he thought she wanted to hear.

"Kunzai, give it to me straight, what did she say?"

"She say: 'Master Eta not at home.'"

Valonga crossed her arms and smiled. Ohhhh, so he wants to play this kind of game, huh?

They listened to the Master's sounds spilling over the wall

for a few more minutes and then strolled away.

"Kunzai, how much money do you make per hour working for the Colonel?"

She had to re-phrase it twice before he understood. There were obviously some drawbacks to being self-taught in English.

He finally understood and gave her a figure.

"Look, I'll double that every evening after you get off from work if you'll come here to Master Eta's house, to translate for me. O.K.?"

"Double?"

"Yes, double."

She could see that she had touched the right chord. Every man had his price. That's a variation on the theme that Armando Bá used to play.

"Remember this, Valonga, if you don' remember nuttin' else, huh? Different people have different rhythms, O.K.? So you can't assume that one person will respond in the same way that another person will respond. You know what I mean? You have to work the rhythms to find what fits."

"So, we come back tomorrow night."

"Yes, tomorrow night."

They strolled out of the Eta district, leaving the pickled smells, the frank odor of fish and rice behind, until tomorrow evening.

She knew she was "different" (as they used to say) by the time she was seven, definitely by the time she was ten. She couldn't explain it and no one could explain it to her. As a member of a solidly middle-class African-American family in Augusta, Georgia, U.S.A., she knew (as well as her mother and father) that her interests were supposed to be somewhat prosaic, almost pedestrian, to be honest. Her interests were not prosaic, never pedestrian; they were always "exotic," different.

She became interested in Capoeira Angola, the bullfight, drums, the Koto, Tae Kwon Do, jazz, writing, The Religion, psychology, African-American politics, African music, spirituality-cosmic, nutrition, photography, Indian music (spirituality), African-American acting, European gourmet cooking, cars-motors-, boxing, our story, the art of braiding, and not necessarily in this order.

When she discovered that she was semi-wealthy and there was a strong possibility that she wouldn't have to hustle her life away trying to earn the basic necessities, she decided to pursue her dream times.

It helped to have parents who could relate to her "bohemianism."

Mother Prince: "Valonga, if it pulls you, go for it!"

Father Prince: "Valonga, I'm a Black man that's done made some money, use what I give you for what's important."

Her father had passed and left her $300,000 solidly entrenched dollars before she had established SMI ("the stress management consultants for international corporations").

She had parleyed the 300 grand into 3 million, appointed a hip group of reliable, upper mobile conscious African-Americans to responsible positions and laid a three year sabbatical on herself.

They related to her adventure because she had made it a part of company policy.

"What sense does it make for us to help others manage stress if we don't have a handle on it ourselves?"

They were Family. She checked in once a week, made important decisions that her second in command couldn't handle and moved...

A number of entrepreneurs had assured her that it wasn't possible to travel and leave a prospering business to subordinates.

"You don't understand, pal, we're friends who happen to be in the business of business together, and we know how to take care of business, they don't need a Valonga Prince standing over them in order to know what to *do* and how to do it."

Three years. Three years. What could you do for three years, within a three year span? Well, you could trip out in the world and "free base" on the heads of those who had something in their heads. The possibility grafted other possibilities onto it and she was off.

She was outside Master Kimio Eta's bamboo walls, trying to gain another kind of understanding.

Kunzai Ozawa, true to his word, stood like a valiant soldier outside the bamboo gate of Eta's home waiting for instructions.

"Kunzai, we have a serious problem here, you understand?"

"Hai, hai, I understand."

She smiled at him affectionately. She was quite certain, after three previous visits to the Master's house, that he clearly understood that they did have a problem.

Visit number one was clearly a bust.

"Master Eta not at home"

Visit number two...

"Master Eta asleep." The sound of Master Eta playing in the background Asleep?

Visit number three...

"Master Eta busy."

The Simian-faced lady opened the gate as before, her face reflecting lights and shadows but giving no clue to her feelings in regards to their intrusion on Master Eta's privacy.

"Kunzai, please tell this lady that my name is Valonga

Prince, I've made three previous visits to this establishment and that I'd like to talk to Master Eta, if that is at all possible?''

Midway through the translation, the Simian-faced lady bowed deeply and performed a two-armed gesture that indicated that they should enter. Welcome.

Kunzai Ozawa matched Valonga's blinks of surprise.

Master Eta met them in his garden with a warm smile, bow and handshake.

She was stunned when he asked in English: "You remember Lay Charles?"

She nodded yes, forgetting that he was blind.

"Uhh, yes, Ray Charles? I do remember him."

He led them through a rice paper panelled room, casually touching an item here and there to orient himself. She decided not to question him about his reluctance to let them into his space on their previous visits.

"Sit, please."

He seated them at a black lacquered table overlooking his garden. Valonga felt transported. So this is a rock garden. She studied the swirl and warf of the raked rock surface, amazed, bewildered and, enchanted by the effect of the arrangement. Kunzai knelt as though he were in a temple.

Master Eta knelt at the table beside them, descending like a calm shadow. He clapped his hands softly, once. The effect was strangely bell-like. Valonga felt she was being transported to a mystical place.

The Simian-faced woman literally oozed onto the scene with a tea tray. Valonga mentally compared her to a snake with a monkey's face.

The tea was poured. They sipped in silence. She looked around the space they were in. The master's koto rested in a corner, looking majestic, musically beautiful.

Chapter 5

"Do not be afraid to be silent. Or to speak, I must return to the Koto in thirty minutes."

He was obviously allowing them to intrude on his practice time. She sipped her tea and stared at the patterns of the rock garden. Thirty minutes later the "monkey woman" appeared, bowed slightly and motioned for them to follow her.

Valonga and her guide stood and bowed to Master Eta. There was nothing else they could do, it seemed. He acknowledged their departing bows with a slight smile, and began to crawl slowly across the floor to his Koto.

Outside the gate, Valonga and Kunzai stared at each other with disbelief. Had they actually been inside the home of Master Eta? Was it a dream?

Two days later, at the same time, she stood outside the gate, dampened by a quiet mist. All of the questions she had wanted to ask the Master during the course of her first, silent visit, bubbled around in her brain.

The simian-faced woman opened the gate slightly, a neutral expression on her face. She bowed and let her in. As before, the master welcomed her and let her to the space facing the garden. She was determined to put it all into perspective this time, to get what she came to Okayama for.

After ten minutes of tea sipping and rock gazing, she was beginning to feel hypnotized by the textural changes caused by the mist settling on the rocks in the garden. It was not or never.

"Master Eta, I must ask you some questions. Do you mind?"

She stared at the serenity of his profile. He could be a living Buddha.

In answer to her question he made a slight bow from the neck and smiled affirmatively. She took another sip of her tea and struggled to force the words of the questions from her head.

The mistiness seemed comfortable, almost a blanket of warmth. She felt drowsy. How can I ask to study the Koto with him? She glanced at the Koto in the far corner of the room, waiting.

The Master's slurping of his tea refocused her attention. He seemed oblivious to her presence.

"Master Eta, I've come from a distant place to be near you, to find out what the Master of the Koto thinks and feels and whether or not you would be willing to teach me?"

The words seemed to echo onto the misted rocks, gently bounce off the walls of the rice paper. Master Eta clapped softly, once, and the woman who served him reappeared with a fresh pot of tea. She smiled at Valonga as she replaced the cold tea pot with a hot one. Valonga smiled back, not understanding why she was suddenly being smiled at. Her words were still circling their space.

"Valonga Prince."

She was startled by the sound of his voice and the full use of her name.

"Yes," she answered timidly.

"I know you have come from a distant place to find out what the master of the Koto thinks..."

She had the feeling that he was mocking her, but the serious expression on his face denied her feelings.

"I know you are interested in the Koto but I do not think you are prepared to go to where the Koto can take you."

She sipped her tea and absorbed the answer, turning it around and around in her head. Does he want me to fight for the right to learn the Koto, or does her really mean what he is saying?

"Master Eta, how can you be so certain about my capabilities?"

He slowly turned to face her, his deadened eyes burning holes into her consciousness.

"Because I am a Master of the Koto."

Silence rang in after his statement, as though a curtain had been pulled down between them. She felt the impulse to argue but couldn't find a handle for her argument. His dead black eyes leveled on her face, forcing her to look away.

"Master Eta, you know I really wanted to study the Koto with you, I really did."

"I know, I know."

He used the silent spaces as well as he used the full notes of the Koto.

"Master Eta, why don't you come out into the world, give the people a chance to experience the beauty of your music?"

He seemed to space out on her question for a moment.

"Valonga, the people have been programmed to ignore the real beauty of music, they only want to hear "noise"."

He spoke quietly and with authority.

"But, but, don't you think the magic of your music would open them up?"

"No, they are gone. It is too late."

"Couldn't you give it a try?"

He released a sad little smile in her direction, and nodded: "No, no, Hiroshima, Washington, D.C."

She felt like arguing the point but decided to forget it. What kind of argument could she use against his logic? Her legs began to ache from being folded under her body, but she couldn't destroy the moment. The ferns and moss clinging to the sides of the rocks seemed to grow greener with each moment. The sound of the Koto pulled her deeper into the natural mysteries in front of her, she became a part of the natural picture window she was looking into. She became a part of the mist sprinkling onto the rocks, she became a part of the landscape receiving the mist.

Am I hallucinating?

The Simian-faced woman slid into peripheral view, signalling, by her presence, that it was time for her to go. Was she his wife?

Valonga stood slowly, awkwardly, like a baby beginning to walk for the first time. Master Eta seemed to be playing a special melody for her departure. She smiled and bowed in his direction. He surprised her by smiling and bowing in return. He must have feelings like radar.

"Sayonora," the woman said in a whispered, musical tone as she closed the gate.

"Sayonora."

Valonga strolled through the narrow streets of Okayama, feeling ebullient, but subdued. It was a strangely personal high. She really couldn't focus on what was making her feel so good, but she knew she had nothing to feel sad about...so...

Finally, completely dampened by the mist she started toward her hotel. She passed Kunzai Ozawa at work and decided not to pop in on him, to exchange chit chat.

What was there to say?

She was up early the next day, prepared to take the train to Tokyo and from there a flight to Seoul, Korea.

The phone ringing at her bedside jarred her.

"Yes, hai?"

"Valonga Prince, this Master Eta..."

"Master Eta?" She sat quietly on the side of the bed.

"I called to wish you success on your journey to learn from the Masters. This is a good thing. I also think you should know that it is not always possible to get what you think you want."

"I understand, Master Eta."

"Sayonara, Valonga Prince."

"Sayonara, Master Eta."

She moved from the bed and stood in front of the window, imagining the view from Master Eta's porch.

"Each time I release a note from my Koto, it is helping to create a harmony in life that did not exist before."

"Come with me, please, the Mae de Santos will see you now."

Valonga followed the man dressed in white thru a narrow passageway, into a bedroom that looked like a cell. The Mae de Santos sprawled on the bed, her head propped up on two snow-white pillows. A small dark woman with sharp, Indian chiseled features, eyes like glowing marbles. Valonga bowed. It seemed to be the right thing to do.

The Mae de Santos pantomimed, "I am tired, I'm not as young as I used to be."

Valonga acknowledged her pantomime-statement with a shrug. Who is as young as they used to be?

61

They stared at each other, smiling, pantomimed conversation spent for the moment. An hour later, Valonga bowed out of the Mae de Santo's presence, stunned by the information she had been given by a person she had never met before.

"You are searching, touring the world, looking for masters, for instruction from masters. I like the idea and I wish you well, my daughter. I think it is very wise that you are here in Bahia with Mestre Juizo, that this should be your base. You are on firm ground here. Eventually you must return to Candomblé you understand?"

Valonga had absorbed the priestess' pantomime, Bahian Portuguese, broken English, understood.

The plane droned hypnotically in her ears, dredging up the memory of Mae de Santos Maria Jose Lima.

I've never been to Candomblé, how can I return?

The Korean coastline appeared. She tabled her own question. Master Yong Bi Kim, Tae Kwon Do master was waiting for her.

"Bow!"

After two weeks she literally yearned for the rhythms of Capoeira Angola. But there was a lot happening with Tae Kwon Do, too. She felt like a superwoman, number one, from doing the most strenuous exercises she had ever done in her life.

"Higher! Kicking, higher!" he shouted at her in his horribly broken English. "I learn English from American soldier after Korean war. I teach them Tae Kwon Do."

Tae Kwon Do, "hand and foot way," Master Yong Bi Kim. The dojang was a barnlike structure with sliding doors on the east and west sides. It was the beginning of the Korean winter and the doors were opened at the beginning of their daily two hours workout and closed at the conclusion.

Valonga couldn't figure it out. She asked one of her

English speaking fellow students: "why are the doors opened?"

"Doors closed in summertime."

She couldn't figure it out.

The belt system was heirarchial and the teaching was tyrannical, no questions, no questions permitted.

"Bow."

They lined up (8 in a rank, 8 in a file), bowed and went to work. Tae Kwon Do meant doing one hundred side kicks with each leg and then 100 more. Simple movements were done exactly, and repeated hundreds of times and repeated. Valonga shared the classes with two other foreigners, one, a German mercenary who had fought for the Boers in South Africa, the other an ex-U.S. soldier from Nebraska. She didn't feel that she had anything in common with either of them.

The German (a Schwarzenegger double), made small talk with her before class from time to time, obviously just to be friendly. The American avoided speaking to her, she guessed, for the same reason. He obviously didn't want to create some kind of ghetto for the two of them, Americans abroad.

"Bow!"

The classes were physically brutal, mentally challenging. How much can your body take? They seemed to be asking.

Master Kim was everywhere.

"Foot should be here, not there!"

Rest periods during the two hour workouts lasted ten seconds each. She challenged every minute of the time she spent in the dojang, and when she hobbled through the streets to her hotel afterwards, her mind seethed with the passion and ice of Tae Kwon Do.

Valonga was surprised to discover that she could hold her own with the others in her belt group (white belts). They were mostly subteenaged children, but they had a tradition of Tae Kwon Do.

She felt like an animal obeying the guttural sounds of her master's voice.

"Bow!"

Her sector of Korea was Tae Kwon Do and painful joints. She felt out of sync with the rigidity of the art, the lack of a rhythm she could easily move with.

She also felt disappointed to discover that the respect for tradition ("bow!"), the will to work through any human obstacle was counterpointed by a racist attitude ("dark people, not good!") and a sexist attitude ("woman need guidance from man").

The first month ended dramatically for her, she was accidentally kicked in the right side and had two ribs broken.

"No problem, go sit down! We fix after class!"

She seriously doubted whether her commitment to Tae Kwon Do would last past the point of her ribs healing. She knelt on the sidelines, (Master Kim insisted that she come to class, even if she was unable to practice) shivering from the wind that blew thru the open doors.

Why don't they close those doors?

She felt that she was learning something about the Korean mentality from watching her classmates work. They seemed to be willing to do anything the Master asked them to do. She became a fascinated observer. The Korean language, except for commands to do this and that, eluded her grasp. But her understanding of what she saw was clear. Each member of the class was a well-oiled cog in the machinery. It seemed that they were all named Kim, Lee, Chang or Han and they gave the appearance of being members of a single family.

Some of the family members struggled harder than others, but they all obeyed. They all obeyed. The realization stunned her one afternoon. The wind was colder and blowing harder now, but the doors remained open. The Korean Autumn.

"The doors are closed in summer."

The dojang became, in some ways, a metaphor for her Korean experience. In the summer, when the doors were open (she imagined), there were fresh green scenes to look at, flowers to smell, a cool wind breezing through.

The doors would be opened onto distractions. The sight of people rioting on television shocked her. The students, in another part of the city, were rioting because several members of their university had been killed by the police.

Valonga looked for some sign, some recognition of what was occurring a few city miles away. There were no signs, it was business as usual. In the dojang.

"Bow!"

The first day she went back to class for practice as usual, she was required to do all of the movements that her classmates had been practicing while she was disabled.

She felt that it was unfair and allowed it to show with an expression of disgust for half the class period. Master Kim asked her to say after class.

"Valonga, I talk with you, stay."

She had learned how to supply the inbetween words that linked questions together. Or made sense of statements that seemed to be strangely worded shorthand. He wanted her to stay after class so that they could talk.

"You are not pleased, huh?"

He stared at a point between her eyes and his question seemed to be more of a statement. She decided to risk everything by answering his statement-question honestly.

"No, Master Kim, I am not pleased."

They knelt on the cold wooden floor of his sparsely furnished "office," facing each other. He cocked his head to one side, as though asking her to tell him why she was not pleased.

Valonga felt a slight panic wedging up in her throat. How can I tell him what I'm displeased about? About the damned doors to the dojang being left open, the brisk-cold Korean wind breezing through? The racist attitude she felt and knew about from observation.

"Dark skin not good!"

The sexism?

"Woman need man to guide them."

Why doesn't someone say something about the riots? Should I say something? The respect for tradition that she felt, that permeated the frosty dojang prevented her from verbalizing her displeasure. It gripped her like a cold flash, this deep Tae Kwon Do, and then it was gone.

Master Kim studied her expression, a sadly comical twinkle in his eyes. There was no need to verbalize it, he had made her understand that Tae Kwon Do was above and beyond ordinary happenings, like riots, racists, cool winds blowing through the open doors.

Tae Kwon Do was the beginning and the end; Master Kim made her understand that without saying a word.

"Valonga, you wish to speak?"

She nodded no and struggled to stand up, her legs cramped from kneeling on the cold floor.

"Bow!" he barked at her as she moved stiffly to leave.

She turned to him, to match his smile with one of her own, and bowed.

"Bow!" was a linchpin for dojang courtesy. Younger students bowed to older students, colored belts bowed to black belts, everyone bowed to tradition.

"Preparation for yellow belt examination next week."

"Yes," she answered and bowed again at the door.

The doors to the dojang were closed, the space empty. It seemed light miles away from Capoeira.

Chapter 6

"Valonga, you are not practicing berimbau as much as you should."

She made an effort to look petulant.

"You are simply playing the rhythm, you are not feeling it." Angola is a rhythm you must feel."

Valonga felt like a real foreigner at the examination.

Master Kim and two assistant instructors sat at the table at the far end of the dojang, underneath a Korean flag. The doors to the dojang were closed, she noticed.

The ranking black belt of her class called out in Korean: "Line up!"

Twenty students immediately took their places. Master Kim stood and slowly walked back and forth through their ranks, inspecting them. They wore the usual ivory white doobok and maintained an at attention stance. He seemed to frown as he looked Valonga from head to toe.

Why did he frown? *Did* he frown? Am I becoming paranoid?

The rioting had escalated, the smell of tear gas drifted from the scene and the television seemed to have it on every channel. But none of it mattered in the dojang.

She alertly followed the preliminaries, the announcements, what this was going to be about, and raced to the sidelines to be seated crosslegged as the examination started.

The examination was to determine whether or not the student would go to the next belt level.

Master Kim was known, even by the Koreans, to be hard. She glanced to her left, mentally calculating the numbers. Five were attempting to go from white belt to yellow, five from yellow to blue, four from blue to green, two from green to brown, two from brown to red and two from red to black.

There's nothing to worry about, she whispered to herself; perform a few kata, do a few kick, bow before and after each cycle, spar with one of her classmates. Or two.

She glanced again to her left. Everyone seems to composed, why am I so nervous? She almost exploded with a sigh of relief when she heard the name of the person next to her called first.

"Kim, Joon Suk!"

Joon Suk Kim ran to a designated place in front of the Master's table and stood at attention. This was the first time she had paid any particular attention to the individuals in the dojang.

They were always kept in line, moving as a unit, until some one goofed. There were periods when everyone seemed to be anonymous, a series of white-suited figures with different colored belts, moving back and forth with brisk, snapping motions.

Joon Suk Kim bowed and, as requested, began to go thru the motions that would mean the difference from remaining

68

a white belt and becoming a yellow belt.

Valonga cringed when she saw the twelve-year-old make his first mistake doing the assigned Kata. Her armpits began to perspire, watching him stop and turn red with embarrassment because he couldn't remember the final movement of the Kata.

One of the assistants barked out an order in imitation Master Kim style and Joon Suk Kim snapped back to attention. The aspiring student had obviously not done well in part one.

Part two was a demonstration of the various kicks. The real beauty of Tae Kwon Do, she felt, were the kicking techniques. The katas, she had decided, were mechanical motions, three steps this way, punch! Four steps that way, kick!

The student started off with a front snap kick! She could tell that his legs were not strong yet but his technique was fine.

He felt more confident after a few kicks and wound up part two with a spinning back kick. The other students sighed with relief. Joon Suk Kim hadn't failed his yellow belt exam, yet.

Free style sparring number three.

"Bi Bin Bap!"

A yellow-belted student scrambled to stand beside Joon Suk Kim, he had been chosen to be his sparring partner, one belt-step higher. They turned away from each other to straighten their doboks and belts, turned back to face each other with uncertain bows and grunted in unison to signal the opening of their sparring match.

Valonga smiled at the sight of the two teenagers circling each other, their fists balled up, looking like small fighting cocks. A sudden mutual flurry of kicks killed her smile. They were seriously trying to kick each other, in the ribs, the chest, the head. She felt like screaming: "Stop! Stop this! Someone is going to get hurt!" Somehow, all of their kicking seemed to be in vain, unfocused, harmless. The sparring match was called to a halt by a barked command.

The two boys arranged themselves, bowed to each other, bowed to Master Kim and stood at attention, breathing heavily.

"Chan Lee!"

Bi Bim Bap bowed quickly and returned to his position on the sidelines. His replacement, Chan Lee, a blue belt, stood at attention, ready to spar with Joon Suk Kim, the aspiring yellow belt.

Valonga subconsciously straightened her back, feeling the pressure that she knew Joon Suk Kim must be feeling. He was obviously tired from sparring with someone slightly more advanced than himself, and now he was being asked to spar with a student who was even more sophisticated.

The same ritual was performed, the straightening up of the dobok, the mutual bowing and the grunt that signaled the beginning of the match. The blue belt was slightly larger and took full advantage of his size. He opened their duel with a front snap kick to Joon Suk Kim's stomach.

Joon Kim was kicked backwards, like a man doing a muscular version of the Michael Jackson "moon walk." He picked himself up and re-entered the kicking zone, three, four, five times. Each time he found himself within kicking range of Chan Lee's front snap kick, he was kicked backwards and to the floor again.

Valonga skipped from feeling sorry for Joon Suk Kim, to feeling a deep sense of admiration for his will to return to the "zone of punishment." The match was called to a halt by another barked command. The two boys, once again, stood at attention in front of Master Kim's table.

He issued a command for them to return to their positions

along the side of the dojang. Valonga took a deep breath and signed.

Master Kim and his assistants compared notes, obviously agreeing on their opinion of Joon Suk Kim.

"Valonga!"

She heard her name as an echo and felt herself floating up from the edge of the mat in slow motion.

"Nao! Nao! Valonga! Don't make your movements quickly. There is time to do quick movements later. Feel the energy of each movement. You unnerstand!"

Black belt Kang spoke to her. He had a reputation for speaking better English than Master Kim, which was completely undeserved.

"Tensen!"

He barked out the kata that Joon Suk Kim had just struggled with, a short time before.

The movements of the kata, the opening forearm defense, the first step in the riding horse stance was mysteriously wiped from her mind for what seemed to be an hour. She refocused on the cynical look in Master Kim's eyes. She could literally hear the wheels in his brain whirl around...another foreigner wanting to study our art, a lazy Black woman.

She was into the middle of the kata before she fully realized it. It was all muscle memory. Three steps forward, middle punch, right, left, kick, punch, right, left, kick, punch. She froze into the attention stance at the conclusion of her kata, feeling elated and slightly paranoid.

What did I leave out? Did I do each movement correctly? Why is Master Kim staring at me like that?

The next section, kicking. Master Kim continued staring at her. She felt uncomfortable, glanced down to discover that her belt had become untied.

She remembered to bow, quickly turned around to re-tie

her belt. Master Kim regarded her attention to neatness with a quick smile.

"Valonga, you are kicking."

She bowed once again and thought of the five basic kicks she felt that she was going well until she stumbled.

It wasn't a terrible mistake, simply a misstep that made her feel awkward and nervous. Each kick had to be done perfectly. She ended her "Kicking" with a brisk front snap kick, and came to attention, slightly winded.

"Once again!" Master Kim called out.

The whole thing once again? Why? What did I do wrong?

Valonga sucked in a deep shot of air, closed her eyes to visualize the kicks in her mind, opened them and began to move. She felt locked into a pattern, on rails, one kick leading to the next one, all interlocked. Her movements were quick, precise. And she didn't stumble.

Once again she finished and stood at attention. Master Kim leaned forward and granted her a smile. Wowww! I must be doing O.K..

"Hoinguk Choi!"

The sparring section. She dreaded it.

Her sparring mate bowed with her to Master Kim, and then they bowed to each other. The guttural growl that exploded from her throat surprised her. She was circling her opponent cautiously, looking for an opening and trying to avoid being kicked or punched. She was fighting. Tae Kwon Do.

The kick she received to her rib cage surprised her more than it hurt, but she realized instantly that something was broken, again.

She felt tempted to stop, to hold her side and collapse, but a glance at Master Kim's smirking face acted as an encouragement for her to continue the bout.

The pain in her side forced her to carefully consider every

move, conserve her efforts, to think. She was surprised to discover weaknesses in her opponent's defense system. She was even more surprised to discover that she was outmaneuvering him and, despite the fact that she wasn't strong enough to deliver a killer kick, she felt that she was holding her own.

It seemed that an hour had passed before Master Kim called the sparring to a halt.

"Stop!"

The opponents bowed to each other, to Master Kim and raced back to half lotus themselves on the sidelines. The pain in Valonga's rib cage sharpened with each breath. But she had completed her examination.

Valonga felt her head wandering again, back to the belt presentation ceremony that took place two weeks after the examination trial. She felt sharp pains in her side with each bow, and there were many to be made.

"Awright, Ms. Prince, stay alive here, this is a writing class, not a siesta hour."

Brother Q., the most serious African-American writer on the scene. She was back in the states, learning how to best put her experiences into some kind of form.

"I *am* alive, Brother O., and believe me I know the difference between a writing class and the siesta hour."

Brother O. flashed a tight little smile in her direction. Not only is she fine, but she's got spunk too. Let's see what her short story is like.

Valonga raked her ballpoint thru the sentences she had just written.

"Truth is, dammit! stranger than any fuckin' fiction, so why not write the truth?"

Chapter 7

The warmth of the circle made her feel at ease, accepted. After weeks, Mestre Juizo was allowing the new students an opportunity to participate in their first roda.

She entered the play with a kind of subdued joy. It was difficult not to be happy, what with the sounds of the Berimbaus and pondieros and songs echoing above them.

She didn't see the sweep coming and for a moment she felt that she was floating in the air, watching her feet sail in front of her eyes.

She landed squarely on her butt, unhurt but shook by the experience. She stood to do the chamada de magin, pleased to be aware of what the next movement should be.

Dinner with Brother O.

She stared up at Brother O.'s face, loving and hating him for what he was doing with them. He made them (all of them, she discovered) realize that America was not the center of the world, and that deeply pissed some of them off.

"You're a fucking radical, Mr. O., if you don't mind me saying so."

"No, Tommy, no, I'm not. I'm an African-American writer living in the U.S. Now lets finish these short stories and forget about what you *think* you understand about my political life."

They were drawn to each other and finally, unable to resist the magnetism, decided to surrender to the Force.

"Mr. O., how about dinner with me tonight?"

"Are you sure you can afford to feed me? I have expensive tastes."

She took him to her favorite Thai restaurant, feeling quite comfortable with his reputation as a womanizer. I'm safe, unless he knows more about Capoeira Angola and Tae Kwon Do that I do.

They ordered bottles of Txing tao, chicken on fire, pad thai, and sprawled back in their seats to look at each other and interweave thoughts.

So, this is the sister whose been everywhere and done everything. Or is going everywhere and doing everything. Hmmmm, Brother O. doesn't seem to be quite as menacing up close as he is in class.

"Valonga—Brother O.?"

They broke into simultaneous smiles. The chilled beer bottles were placed in front of them.

"I will bring your meal shortly."

"You were about to say?"

"No, ladies first."

She rolled her eyes at him, a burlesqued caricature of the coquette.

"If you insist, kind sir?"

"I insist."

"I'm curious about you, about the life of a writer. Who were you before you became Brother O. and why?"

"You get right to the point, don't you? I had no idea that you were taking me to dinner to pump me?"

"I'm sure you must've had some suspicions that I was interested surely."

"Well, why no tit for tat?"

"What do you want to know?"

Their opening gambit—mutual interrogation—was interrupted by the waitress bringing their food.

"Your dinner is served."

"Mmmmm, looks good."

"And, as you see, it's not terribly expensive."

"Well, as Dad used to say: "Some of the best things in life don't cost anything.""

They semi-surprised each other by being expert chopsticks users.

"God, don't you just hate people who use chopsticks and don't know how?"

"You just put your finger on one of my favorite peeves."

They took the edge off their hunger pangs with a few mouthfuls of food and started back into their conversation.

"You were about to tell me about yourself."

"I was?"

She decided that she liked him. She liked the gleam in his eye, his lack of pretension, his way of sparring with her.

"Yes, you were."

"It'll cost you another beer. And remember, tit for tat."

"You got it."

He felt a tinge of chauvinism watching her signal to the waitress. It wasn't his thing, usually, to allow himself to be taken out by women, but he had felt the urge to approach Valonga in a different way.

He took a long sip of his beer and enjoyed a few bits of

his food, pretending that he had forgotten her question.

"You were about to tell me about yourself, have you reneged?"

She was obviously serious. It was time for him to become serious.

"Yes, you were about to tell me how a writer is made."

He took another long sip of his beer before answering.

"Well, I have to say, first off, that I think writers are born, not made."

She spurred him on with a quizzical expression. He smiled at her subtle prompting.

"I know a lot of people wouldn't agree with me on this but, what can I say? It's my opinion."

"I know for certain that it isn't possible to write if you don't have the talent and the talent isn't something that can be designed."

"What about writing classes? I mean...you..."

"Mostly ripoffs, group therapy sessions. Yes, even mine. I know that there is a ninety percent likelihood that most of the people who come into my class will never develop into writers because they don't have the talent for it."

"Explain that a little more."

"Simple. Children who've learned the alphabet can write, but that doesn't make writers out of them. Let me give you my definition of what a writer is, what a writer does..."

She signalled the waitress for another round. His eyebrows wiggled his approval. He made a silent toast to her with the fresh bottle of beer.

"As you probably know by now, a writer is a very, very special sort of creature. As an artist he/she becomes closest to being like a bullfighter than any other creature in the world that I can think of."

Valonga leaned forward on the table, her Bad Thai temporarily forgotten.

"I know that strikes a lot of people in a weird way."

"What makes you see it that way, make that kind of analogy?"

A film flared briefly in her brain. Manuel Arruza, "Machete" flashed a smile, whirled a gorgeous red cape across the back of her brain and was gone.

I wonder if "Machete" would equate Bullfighting to writing?

"Are you familiar with the bullfight?"

"Yes, strangely enough, I know quite a bit about the corrida."

"Good, then I can get as technical as I want to get. Like I said, the writer, like the bullfighter, is a special sort of creature. The bullfighter comes to his art with a cape and a sword, the writer with a pencil and an eraser, in the old-fashioned sense of the word.

"The writer has a beginning, middle, and an end and he, too, faces death at every stage of the game. Of course, as you know, one of these artists is apt to be dealing with a more immediate death each time he goes into the arena."

They exchanged conspiratorial smiles, was he talking about the bullfighter or the writer?

"O.K., now that I've taken you into the analogy, lets leave the matador out of it for a bit."

She felt the vaguest impulse to pull her notebook and ballpoint out of her totebag.

"The writer is this reckless creature with all the brains who is willing to take on one of the most savage beasts the world has ever known, the blank page!"

Valonga nodded vigorously, recalling her first week in Brother O.'s class.

"No matter how well-armed the writer is, that blank sheet of paper can be the most dangerous, most intimidating factor he will ever have to deal with.

"As you know, from reading the Masters, the real monster in the bullring is not the bull, but the crowd. That's the way I feel about writing; the real monster is not the pen and paper, but you. You are your worst enemy, the real monster."

"At the beginning of your story, your play, article, novel, or whatever, many have slaughtered themselves without really knowing that that's what they were doing. Needless to say, what I'm referring to is something called the beginning. I've seen strong men and brave women go down in defeat, right at the beginning. They, obviously, are not writers. The writer would never surrender at the beginning, the beginning is going to make or break you. That's something we all realize and have to be prepared for."

"Were you sure of yourself when you first confronted the monster?"

"Yes, I was. I knew, intuitively, that I was going to be the master of the situation. No doubt about. But that's the way the writer—matador—must think about the situation."

"And your faena, that middle section that forces you to put your best moves out there, what about that? Were you still in control?"

Brother O's eyes misted over for a moment.

"Yes, I gotta say yes. I don't know what it was that took me to the right place, helped me make the right moves. But it was there and I knew it. There were times when I felt like the old time greats who used to ask the people in the arena, after he had performed some spectacular movements, 'am I not Unique?'"

"You're talking about Carlos Arruza."

Brother O. fixed her face in his cross-hairs, looked as though he were lining her up for a moment of truth.

"Shit! You really do know something about Bullfighting, don't you?"

"I told you. Please, go on."

Valonga saw a glitter shine up in Brother O's eyes. Was it the effect of the beer or the excitement of talking about "his craft?"

"Yes, that's the feelings of being unique. The honest people will always admit to that. It's like you're doing something in the world that nobody else even thought about doing."

The restaurant had cleared out, leaving them the afternoon to talk and drink beer.

"And the ending, the moment of truth? How does that fit your analogy?"

He took a moment to line his words up, to profile his answer.

"Now that's really where the analogy hits the nail on the head."

She sprawled in her seat, watching him become the bullfighter who wanted to make the perfect kill.

"If everything has been done exceptionally well, up to this point, it is always possible to blow the whole deal with an inept ending."

"How do you guard against that?"

"To be honest, I'd have to say that I don't think it's possible to guard against that particular demon, I've often had the feeling that the ending, the kill, is something that's determined by forces outside of ourselves."

"That's a strange statement. I mean, we've been dealing with the writer as a creator, as one who has control of things and suddenly you're taking me into spirits 'n stuff. C'mon, now, Brother O! Are you pulling my leg?"

They shared the smile for a moment.

"Valonga, I know it sounds weird, but believe me, I'm not joking. It would be easy to say that the writer is in complete control, from beginning to end, but I don't happen to feel that way. The ending, for me, is a kind of unusual death sense. And no one really knows how they're going to die.''

''But what about this craft you're talking about, the right way to do this or that?''

''Read my lips. That's what I'm saying . . . there comes a point, the end that no amount of skill or intelligence can control. It's like death happening and no one can predict when that's going to happen, when, or why.''

''The bullfighter can.''

''You wanna bet?''

Chapter 8

She stared out over the blue-green waters of Lake Michigan from her tenth floor apartment. It was nice to have friends who would trip off for vacations and leave their condos in your care for a couple of weeks.

She stirred the ballpoint around above the paper, undecided about her approach to the story she wanted to create.

"Valonga, remember, in Capoeira Angola, in life, you must allow the movement to flow. You unnerstand?"

She smiled, picturing Mestre Juizo standing in front of the group of perspiring students, his arms folded across his chest, his eyes gleaming like marbles.

Let it flow, huh?

Valonga stared at the sentence as though she were reading words written by someone else.

Let it flow, huh?

"How was I to know, when I started on my trip, that I

would be entering worlds I had only dreamt about?"

A "Georgia Peach" from a good family, the recipient of the best vibes money could never buy. My mother said: "go for it, Valonga, go for it!" and my father, bless his sweet soul, died and left me enough money to do exactly that.

Valonga Prince, entrepreneur, stress management consultant to corporations, filled to the brim with stress, money.

What started me on the trip, what impulse took hold of me, made me want to study Capoeira Angola, get into the bullfight, study the conga in Cuba with Armando Bá, beg to study the Koto with Eta, get my ribs kicked in by Tae Kwon Do, do what I'm doing?

She left her place in the breakfast nook to pour herself a glass of sherry in the living room. The lake shimmered in the near distance, small boats saddled the waves, it seemed dreamlike.

She wandered around the room, examining the things she had examined three days before, the giant avocado trees, the African stools and masks.

What's real? What is a dream? What's unreal?

Let it flow, huh?

She replenished her sherry glass and returned to the table and notebook in the breakfast nook.

"There are moments in Capoeira Angola when everything comes into play, the muscles, the mind, the primitive, the sophisticated, cruelty, warmth, life, the possibility of death, all counterpointed by the music of the Berimbas, pandiero, atabaque, agogo and recoreco.

"The 'game' becomes a reflection of everything that any human being will have to face in this life. The 'game' becomes life. Sometimes it's sweet, like honey is sweet, at other times it's bittersweet, like cocoa with no sugar in it. But, like life, it is never completely bitter, no matter what they try to make us believe.

"Life cannot be bitter. 'How's that for a statement?'"

She stopped writing for a minute, flushed with the egotism of being capable of making a definitive statement.

"Manuel Arruza, 'Machete,' said to me one day on a sun-drenched balcony in Andalusia: 'In the corrida, in life, there are no losers. Some of us may have more than others as we go on, but we all start off drawing in air, breathing, filling our lungs up with precious air. Later, much later, we think of filling our pockets with gold.'

"Mestre Juizo, Armando Bá, Kimio Eta, Yong Bi Kim, and all the rest of the wisest men and women that I've met in this world have said the same thing.

"What is this about? My trip? What I've heard and paid attention to, the meaning of life to me. I can't really say, truthfully, what this is about. All I can see in front of me is a voyage that I must take.

"Art, writing, life, music, singing, the dance, all of the elements..."

Valonga carefully placed her ballpoint inside her notebook and closed it. She took a sip from her glass and made a meditative stroll into the living room, to stare, once again, out onto the waters of the lake.

Let it flow, huh?

I can't write. I can't scribble out feelings that are so deep that they won't allow themselves to be placed on blank sheets of paper.

"The real monster is not the pen and paper, but you. You are your worst enemy, the real monster."

Fuck you, Brother O.!!

Valonga glared out of the window, a trickle of tears sliding down her cheeks. Who in the hell wants to write? Why should I force myself to try to put words on paper that're supposed to spell out how I feel about life, about anything?

She wandered back into the kitchen, opened her notebook and stared at the page she had been writing on.

I'm not a writer. I can spell pretty good, and I know past from present tense, and I'm not a writer. Or am I?

She slammed the notebook closed and leaned against the kitchen sink, feeling morose, melancholic, evil.

Is that what writers go through? Damn...

Under the circumstances she felt the best thing for her to do was to have her hair braided.

"Yes, it's going to take at least eight hours for the style you want."

They called her Malana, the Braider, and she was known by no other name.

"Malana, you mind if I ask you some questions while you work?"

"We can talk, I'm not into being interrogated."

Valonga studied their images in the large mirrors surrounding them on three sides. She, sitting in the barber's chair and the slender, small featured, dark-skinned woman combing her hair out to be braided.

Malana felt Valonga's head, recording the surface with her fingers. She knew, after a few minutes, what style of braiding she intended to design.

"Malana, you have quite a reputation, you know?"

"Yes, I know."

Valonga stared into the blind woman's eyes as she began to braid her hair from the back.

She was obviously not given to idle chatter. Valonga settled into a relaxed state, absorbed by the intricate rhythms she felt happening to her head.

The Braider was carefully creating a basket weave on each side of her head, with six corn rows striping the middle.

"How do you feel?" Malana asked, an hour into her work.

Valonga heard the words, knew what they meant but couldn't answer. She nodded, glancing at the figure in the triple layer of mirrors that surrounded her. She studied the figure in the mirror, felt puzzled, but not surprised to see herself sitting in the barber's chair. Where was Malana?

She felt a gentle, wavy feeling wash over her head, something pulling her into a deep sleep.

Valonga and Malana, the Braider, held hands as they stepped over the sleek black body of the leopard gracefully sprawled across their path.

"Valonga, don't be afraid of anything here. The animals won't bite you, the people won't lie to you, and when we leave you'll have some idea of how people should really live together."

Two suns bathed their naked bodies with a buttery light. The tall sheaves of lush black grass that brushed against their bodies felt like massages. People of all colors played around them, to the left and right of them, walked together, sang beautiful songs, sprawled on mini-oasis shaped patches of ground, feeding lions, tigers, wolves and other animals of prey, tidbits of food. Nude.

Malana gently tugged Valonga's hand, pulling her to a place beside her as she sat down beside a ribbon of liquid that moved as slowly as a fast glacier.

The warmest, gentlest breeze Valonga had ever felt caressed her body.

"Valonga, how do you feel?"

"I feel beautiful, I feel wonderful, lovely, sensual, gorgeous. I can't understand it."

"There is nothing to understand, just simply relax and dream."

Valonga looked into Malana's eyes, took note of the glitter.

"Malana, are...are you still blind, here in this place?"

The Braider's face was swallowed up by a sly smile.

"I wasn't blind in the other place, I simply couldn't see."

Large and small birds, gorgeously feathered, fluttered onto the trees near them. The sun's maintained a constant warmth, never too hot. It would be beautiful to have a man right now, someone who was sensitive and honest and loving...

Malana moved slightly away from her side as the man cradled Valonga in his arms. He kissed her as though he were sipping nectar from a flower. They caressed each other; she was woman and he was man and there were no questions to be asked.

After hours of making slow-motion love, after the mutual exchange of love feelings, the man stood up and backed away from her, smiling, leaving her with a perfect memory.

She didn't feel the urge to know him beyond the point that they had been together. It had been perfect, no need to spoil it with any emotions beyond the ones they had shared.

Malana seemed to flow back into Valonga's field of vision, her body steaming from a brief dip in the river.

"A word of caution, Valonga; you can get what you wish for here, if the vibe is right."

They spent hours lolling on the river bank, eating berries and other fruit from low-hanging trees.

"Malana, who owns this place?"

"We do, Valonga, we do, and we have never had a war."

The Braider beckoned for her to follow. She slowly stood up, fascinated by the sight of two lions playing a game of tag with a herd of Springboks.

An involuntary shiver rippled down her back, recalling the horror scenes of the killer lions lunging onto the backs of the deer, in long ago scenes from the "Wild World of Animals."

"They don't do that here," Malana spoke softly, following the direction of her eyes, reading her mind. They walked through the black grass, stopping to smell, taste, admire, watch. After a half mile, Malana pointed to the thatched huts of a tiny village.

"Looks like everyone is here for a change."

As they approached the village, men, women, and children of all colors and races streamed out to greet them, laughing and smiling.

"Malana, welcome back! Where've you been so long?!"

"Who is your beautiful friend?!"

Valonga felt a warm flush race through her being. The people were so natural, so warm, so human. No one frowned, looked malevolent or acted inhumanly.

"How do you feel, Valonga?"

She stared at the images of herself and Malana, the Braider, in the mirrors that corralled them on three sides.

"I feel as though I've been dreaming. Have I been dreaming?"

"Maybe you have and maybe you haven't."

Brother O. rubbed the stubble of his chin, absently scratched his forehead, smiled as he read her story.

"And you say this happened while you were having your hair braided? Beautifully done, I might add."

"Yes, while I was having my hair braided. Thanks for the compliment."

He flashed an absentminded smile in her direction and re-read her story. Twenty minutes later he was giving her a few fine points to consider.

"Valonga, don't trip on what I'm saying, these are just fine line points I'm making. You're a writer, no doubt in my mind. But what you have to do is use your writing muscles more. It's a lot like that Capoweera you talk about."

"Capoeira."

"You know what I mean. If you don't work it, it doesn't become functional. I think what you need to do, frankly, is get into a subject you feel strongly about and go for it. You got anything in mind?''

They exchanged knowing smiles as he made a slow advance and she backed away, fending his advance off with the edges of her palms.

Valonga bent lower as he tried to mesh the music of Capoeira Angola into the slight sway that the boat forced into her ginga.

"Valonga, pay attenshun! The ginga is very important for Capoeira Angola, maybe the most important.''

Mestre Juizo demonstrated the simple steps of the ginga again and again.

"Like this, you see? Close to the ground, lower!''

His ginga, a simple stepping forward and stepping backward, in perfect time to one of the rhythms of Capoeira Angola, was elegant.

In the beginning her thigh muscles surrendered to fatigue, and slowly grew stronger, able to stand the bent position for half hour at a time.

"Do the ginga as *your* movement. You understand? The ginga is different for each because each of us is different.''

She felt comfortable doing the movements she had been taught; the meia lua, the besoa, the au, the rastiera.

It was 11:00 a.m. and she had the mirrored ballroom to herself, by arrangement with the chief steward.

"You want to practice dance? Yes, of course, you may use the ballroom. We will only make use of it three times during our voyage, in the evening.''

She made a slow cartwheel, looking at her image upside down as she made the movement.

"Where are you going now, Valonga?''

"I'm going for a cruise, to write a book.''

"But why take a cruise? Why not stay here with me and

write, you know I'll give you all the help I can."

"Brother O., I know you mean well, but as you've often said, you have to do what you have to do."

"Bon voyage."

This was her second practice session in as many days. She felt loose, but tight like a spring.

God, wish I had someone to practice with. She continued her workout, alternating fast and slow movements, becoming lost in the motion of her muscles.

The man sitting in a chair on the left side of the ballroom floor startled her. He was dressed in white and looked mysterious.

Chapter 9

The Anabacoa was registered to Liberia, Greek owned and was taking a seven day voyage to Acapulco.

Valonga stepped into the ballroom, stashed her gym bag in a corner, made a surreptitious panlook around the room for stray persons and began her workout.

She was filmed with sweat after a half an hour and paused to towel her face and neck.

There he was, in his usual place, dressed in white. She nodded in his direction, the nervous reaction of a familiar stranger. He absorbed her nod and moments later, made a dry nod in return. And remained in place, watching her.

Valonga reversed the tape and made an effort to create variations on each movement she had made in the first half hour. She felt self-conscious, as though she were performing in front of a critical audience of one.

He stayed for the course of her hour and a half workout

and strolled out as she was toweling the sweat off at the end.

That evening he bent over her left shoulder at the Captain's table and spoke to her for the first time.

"The seat next to you is empty; may I sit there?"

"Yes," she nodded.

"My name is Juan Rojo Diablo and you are Valonga Prince."

She felt twinges of nervousness sitting next to the man who had been watching her workout.

He knew her name, that was easy, he had asked one of the stewards.

"I like your Capoeira Angola."

She felt as though someone had poured a hot glass of water down her back. What did he know about Capoeira Angola? Why didn't he say Capoeira Regional? That's what most people knew.

"Oh, are you a Capoeirista?

"I have done some of that in my time, yes, also Tae Kwon Do, Hap Kido and Tai Chi."

"You're a martial artist?"

"Those elements are a part of my life experience, but I could never call myself a martial artist, I lack the discipline for that calling."

Their budding conversation was interrupted by the waiters placing beautifully grilled plates of huachinango Ala. Vera Cruzana in front of them. She surreptitiously studied the man's profile, in between bites of the succulent red snapper.

One of those "International looking types." He could be Brazilian. An Arab maybe. A mulatto from Haiti. He talks strangely, somehow, almost formally. Very manly looking man. Really handsome. Not Hollywood handsome, but really handsome in the way that a man should be handsome. About forty-five, a young fifty. Five feet ten, ten-and-a-half, trim. He must exercise a lot. Why the white suits?

"You are trying to guess my race?"

He turned towards her, his left eyebrow hooked into a humorous question mark.

His eyes seem to be dark green. Or is it the light in here?

"It's not so much your racial background that I'm interested in, to be honest, it's why you've been watching me work out everyday. That's what I'm interested in."

His smile is delicious, just the right blend of cynic; optimist, romantic.

"I am interested to see you work out because the movements of Capoeira Angola are so reverent, so filled with spirituality, so deep."

His answer started her but left her feeling slightly dissatisfied. She *did* want to know about him racially, also.

His gaze was direct, disconcerting, patient.

"I can see that you understand a lot about Capoeira Angola. Now then, let's get the racial thing out of the way."

He took a sip of wine and made a delicate burp before answering.

"I consider myself a world person. I hold a Dominican passport. My parents on my mother's side were African-Spanish-French-Portuguese-Italian. On my father's side, Albanian Gypsy, Arab-African-Armenian."

"I can see why you'd consider yourself a "world person."

Once again he smiled at her. She felt that he was sharing a neatly packaged secret.

They simultaneously turned their attention to the other people at the table. They were fifteen altogether, two couples and eleven singles.

She had been surprised to be invited to have dinner at the Captain's table every evening.

"It is a custom on the Anabacoa for single passengers to sit at the Captain's table. It is not required, of course."

It seemed to be an intelligent idea and she bought into it.

95

It was obviously better to join a group than occupy a table alone, pretending to read a novel. Novels. The cruise was going to clear her head for a novel. She had the beginning and middle of "Nelson Pratt." It was going to be a composite of Nelson Mandela and Geronimo Pratt. It was going to be a 300 page work detailing the plight of political prisoners in the United States.

"Have you been to Acapulco before, Miss Prince?"

"No, no, I haven't."

They exchanged eye signals and smiled at the sight of the lustful couple across from them. They had escalated from being a single man and woman, in two days, to being a hot breathing duo with hands that constantly roved over each other's bodies.

"I don't think you will like Acapulco very well."

She was decidedly undecided about how to feel about him. She liked his charm, the coolness of his approach, but she felt uneasy about his goals. What was he after? A sexual conquest? A chance to say: "I put another notch on my 'gem' during the cruise to Acapulco?"

They smiled at each other over the after dinner coffee and cognac.

"If you are not going to your cabin, may I ask you to join me in a stroll around the ship?"

Valonga felt the urge to laugh. This is like something on T.V., what was that fluffhead program called? "The Loveboat."

They strolled around the upper deck of the Anabacoa, sipping cognac.

"Have you been on many cruises, Mr. Diablo?"

"Please, don't be so formal, please call me Juan and I will call you Valonga."

"O.K., fine, well, have you...?"

They paused near the stern and leaned over to stare at the

96

odd sight of the moon gobbling up the bubbles trailing their ship.

She felt he was being slightly too theatrical when he answered: "Yes, I have been on many cruises, many voyages, sometimes I think, too many."

She stared at his profile in the moonlight, the ship's lights striking the odd planes of his face.

He looks like an ancient Egyptian pharaoh.

"Yes, too many voyages," he murmured more to himself than to Valonga, and then suddenly turned to her with a bright smile.

"And what will you do in Acapulco?"

She suddenly felt embarrassed to be caught studying his profile, to be thinking of him

"I...I'm going to work on a novel."

She liked the quizzical hook that forked his left eyebrow up.

"But, I thought you were a Capoeirista, an Angoliero."

"I'm working on that, and the novel too."

"You are a woman of amazing talents."

She decided not to ask if he were joking or not. They continued their stroll, passing couples with their arms linked around each other, moonstruck.

They strolled in step, silently for awhile.

"And what will you be doing in Acapulco, Mr. Diablo?"

"Please, Juan..."

"Juan."

"In Acapulco, nada. The cruise is only for the sake of giving me a few days to think, to relax my brain, take a break from the fast lane."

"Is your line of work that stressful?"

The little voice whispered softly: "Careful, Valonga, the stress management consultant in you is beginning to surface."

"I am an archaeologist and, to some, it might not seem stressful, but when you've been working on a project for a number of years it can cause a bit of a problem."

An archaeologist? She didn't know whether to believe him or not.

"Are you currently dealing with a project?"

"Yes, as a matter of fact, I am. I'm taking a few weeks off right now, but the project concerns our investigation into the importance the quilombos of Brazil ... those settlements of escapees from slavery."

"Ohhhh I see, so that's how you know so much about Capoeira Angola."

He made a slight, mocking bow.

"We are learning more and more all the time."

They spontaneously clinked their empty cognac glasses together.

"Would you like to have a nightcap with me, a refill?"

"No, thank you, it's been a full evening for me already."

"Are you practicing tomorrow morning?"

"As close to ten o'clock as possible."

"Perhaps I could join you."

She couldn't conceal her surprise.

"To work out, to practice Capoeira Angola?"

He smiled roguishly.

"I have been mentally practicing with you and I'm not too much out of condition."

"I didn't mean to imply ... "

"I understand. Ten a.m. in the ballroom?"

"Sure, yes, see you in the morning."

He had left her at the entrance-hallway to her stateroom.

"Goodnight, Valonga, sweet dreams."

"Goodnight, Juan."

After hours of making slow motion love, after the mutual

98

exchange of love feelings, he, the man, stood up and backed away from her, smiling, leaving her with a perfect memory.

She didn't feel the urge to know him beyond the point that they had been together. It had been perfect, no need to spoil it with any emotions beyond the ones they had shared.

Malana seemed to flow back into Valonga's field of vision, her body steaming from a brief dip in the river.

"A world of caution, Valonga, you can get what you wish here, if the vibe is right."

Valonga slowly opened her eyes and stared through the porthole above her bed. Juan Rojo Diablo was the man she had made love to, on her fantasy—dreamtrip—with Malana, the Braider. She felt absolutely certain that he was the man.

She sat up in bed and wrapped her arms around her knees. Juan Rojo Diablo is the man that I made love with in a dream. How did he?...What's he doing here...?

She sprawled back in bed, staring at the mocking face of the moon, remembering the gentleness of the man, the complete satisfaction he had given her.

A half-hour later she climbed out of bed, unable to sleep, opened her notebook and worked on the outline for "Nelson Pratt."

They nodded formally to each other, their images reflected in the ballroom mirrors. She tried to conceal the strange feelings she had about him, about what they had shared. Or had they?

Valonga placed a tape of Mestre Juizo singing his composition, "Eu Angola," in the cassette. Valonga felt proud of being a member of the chorus that was made up of students from the Academia Capoeira Angola.

The beautifully liquid music of the Mestre's berinbau and voice took them quickly through a warm up. They opened up their movement section with music from Mestre Pastinha's

Academia. The profound sweep of the music forced them to perform low movements, to do their graceful gingas in a crouch. They were absorbed by the feelings of Capoeira Angola, but carefully studied each other peripherally.

How smooth and clear his movements are.

So much grace, her ginga is lovely...

After a separate period of practice, they subconsciously fell into a reda. Suddenly they were playing each other, matching stamina and intelligence in a physical chess game. Valonga made a conscious effort to remember every instruction Mestre Juizo had given her.

"Don't be in a hurry, feel the movement!"

"Be exactly precise, don't aim your kick everywhere, be precise."

Chamada de Magin, rastiera, meia lua, cabecada, au, au, giratorio, besoa...Juizo.

They came to a spontaneous halt and shook hands, breathless and bathed with sweat.

"You play well, Valonga, very well."

"And so do you, Juan."

They were stunned by the applause that erupted from the half dozen passengers who had filtered in while they were playing.

He smiled at her.

"You see, they also approved of your Capoeira Angola."

They toweled the sweat from their faces, feeling loose, clean from the exercise.

"Valonga, will you have lunch with me?"

"Sorry, Juan, I've got homework to do."

She had already decided to place a distance between them. She felt uneasy about him, somehow. He *was* the man she had known in her trip with Malana. But there was a distinction. This man seemed to want something, the man in the other place shared only a memory.

He made another semi-formal bow before they parted in front of the ballroom entrance, and went his way without another spoken word.

"Gosh, that was really some wonderful stuff you guys were doing. What's it called?"

Valonga looked into the bubbling, freckled faces of the twins questioning her and made a spontaneous decision.

"It's called Capoeira Angola, and if you're her tomorrow morning at 10 a.m., I'll give you your first and only lesson!"

"Wowww! Gee, thanks! We'll be here!"

The twins scrambled away. Valonga made a meditative stroll to her cabin. Good. I need company around with this man.

She showered and lay face down on her bed. The game that they had played was different from any she had ever experienced. He had cut off her movements, at times, as though he could read her thoughts and knew exactly where she was going to move next. She shivered, remembering how closely they had worked together, how closely they had played together.

I'll have to find out who his Mestre was. "Nelson Pratt" claimed her attention for the afternoon.

She fell into a deep sleep, feeling the pressures of the bars around her. She was "Nelson Pratt" in solitary, licking her wounds after a four hour torture session with members of the "Security Detachment."

Valonga felt certain that "Nelson Pratt" would have an uphill struggle for publication.

Who wants to suggest that the U.S. has or ever had political prisoners? And that they've been tortured.

Mentally, she reviewed the J. Edgar Hoover era, the Bush CIA administration, the assassinations, shootouts, dirty tricks, sneaky tricks to squelch legitimate grievances against

101

racism, discrimination, sexism and sheer political complaints.

How can I write what is common knowledge (for some people) and not seem hypocritical by saying I love America? Why in the hell did I pick this subject to deal with?

"The writer should make every effort to tell the truth, as he/she sees it, that's all that anyone expects of you."

She scribbled a note to herself to write Brother O., to tell him that she was going into her first novel. That she was really trying to tell the truth. I'm sure he'll be pleased to hear that.

By dinner time, she felt lightheaded with hunger and the modern history of all the political repressions she could casually recall.

"The first political prisoners in this land of the free and home of the brave were probably Black."

The outline was done, she had a beginning, middle and end, complete with rising action, climax and resolution. It was time for dinner.

Diablo signalled for her to occupy the seat to his right. He had placed her name on a card and propped it against a water glass.

"I didn't know we were allowed to reserve seats at the Captain's table."

"We are allowed to do whatever we can get away with," he whispered.

Valonga flushed warm, felt turned on by the way he spoke to her.

"And what do we want to get away with?"

He winked and lifted his wine glass to share a toast with her.

The night air was lush with pleasant smells, the ocean calm, mysterious. They strolled the deck, cognac glasses held at port arms.

"We are close to Acapulco, another night and we will be

there.''

They paused in the same place they had stopped the night before.

"Juan, I'm curious about something . . ."

He cocked his eyebrow at her, expecting a question with the expression.

"Juan?"

"Yes?"

"I know that may seem like a silly cliche, but have we ever met, have we ever known each other before?"

The quizzical expression surrendered to a calm, serious, but strangely mysterious look. He gently took her glass and placed both of their drinks on a nearby tray.

"Yes, yes, we have known each other," he said as he scooped her into his arms, "and I can't begin to tell you how happy I am to be with you again."

Valonga embraced Juan, holding her body against his as though they were dancing in place. She stared into the distance beyond his neck, shivering from the experience.

"Where did we know each other before?" she asked in a small, far away voice.

"You remember, I'm sure you do," he replied, and kissed her.

The kiss did it. With her eyes closed she could imagine the beautiful place Malana, the Braider, had taken her. The delightful atmosphere, the peacefulness.

She didn't want to believe that she was there again, with the man. But she was. And once again, they were naked, creating waves of exquisite pleasure for each other.

The sky was streaking with shards of gold and silver light when he quietly removed himself from her bed, smiling.

"Remember," he reminded her, "you promised to give two little girls a Capoeira Angola lesson."

She nodded, her senses washed by a dreamy attitude.

"I will too, a promise is a promise."

He disappeared without a trace. She woke up two hours later, cradled her head in her hands and tried to recall the specifics of what had happened. They had made love for hours, but she felt between her legs and couldn't feel any evidence of it. She turned to stare at the pillow next to her, and had no sign that a head had pressed it, the chair next to the bed, where he had lain his clothes, no sign.

And yet, she felt completely satisfied. She wanted to see him, to tell him that she loved him, that she loved the feeling he created in her.

Chapter 10

The Capoeira Angola lesson for the twins had been a good experience for all of them.

She forced herself to recall Mestre Juizo's teachings.

"Do only this much, not the big movement." And, "feel how special the movement is."

They were good students and at the end, sweatstained and loose from an hour of workout and instruction, she felt the urge to play but Juan wasn't there and he was the only one she could play with.

Wonder where he is?

They were docking Acapulco the next day, at noon.

Wonder where he is?

He wasn't at lunch. She prowled the ship, casually searching for him. He wasn't at dinner. She felt betrayed, deserted. She wandered around the ship, her fists dug into the pockets of slacks.

She finally discovered him, standing in the place they shared their first kiss. He greeted her calmly.

"Good evening, Valonga."

She felt the urge to ignore him; to keep moving, but she knew that would spell out emotional fraud on her side. She decided to go "for real."

"Juan, I've been looking for you all day. Where have you been?"

"I was in my cabin, I had letters to write."

She felt relieved. At least he hadn't made a "one night" stand of it. She stood next to him, feeling young, foolish, loving. He stared out at the ocean.

"Valonga, you are like me, a nomadic spirit..."

She felt, once again, the strange sense of having known him in another place.

"We were, a long time ago, in another place, lovers."

Valonga stared at his ancient profile, pleased to know that they had been lovers, but disturbed. How could we have been together in a place that was a dream?

He smiled at the confusion she reflected and gently pulled her into his arms. She shivered, suddenly chilled by the feeling of being in the arms of a man who didn't really exist.

"You know my secret, Valonga. You are one of the few with the knowledge of my secret."

He kissed her and she trembled, her eyes held hysterically open, unable to enjoy the moment.

What have I gotten myself into?

She felt weak, incapable of resisting the gentle tug of a hand around her waist, taking her to his cabin.

He was a "dream lover," a title one of her girlfriends had coined. She felt no sensation of being penetrated, it was as though he had always been there, kissing her, loving her, inside of her.

Orgasmic waves washed over her, some starting from the

back of her neck and going to the back of her knees, others circled her waist with peristaltic motions. She came endlessly, a rich flow of pleasure-butter.

The next morning she awoke in her own bed, feeling disoriented.

"Juan?"

She showered, dressed in cool cotton white and strolled onto the main deck. The Anabacoa was gliding into the port of Acapulco.

"Senorita, pardon me, I have a message for you."

Valonga felt the strength drain out of her as the steward handled her the thin envelope.

"Dearest Valonga, I truly thank all of the Forces in this world, and the Other World, the place that I am from, for allowing us to meet and share love again."

She held onto the note with both hands, trying to prevent her hands from shaking.

"I thought, briefly, of asking you to go back with me, but I realized how unfair that would be to you, for you. There are things you have to do and I cannot be guilty of altering your fate. Love, Juan Rojo Diablo."

She stumbled around the ship in a daze for an hour, half looking for Juan and half praying that she wouldn't find him.

After two days and nights in the hedonistic atmosphere of the Acapulco Hotel she was ready to move on. There was something essentially silly about the activities of the people who could afford to play around in the sand.

She "released" the presence of Juan Rojo Diablo from her head.

As a stress management expert she knew it was important for her mental safety to "release."

What have I got to hold on to anyway?

She was in Mexico City and into the third chapter of "Nelson Pratt" before she fully realized it. This is the perfect place to get into a piece like this.

Mexico City was bursting at the seams with people, feverish activity, games.

"Pardon me, Senõrita."

"Senõra."

"Yes, of course, Senõra. My name is..."

"Yes, I recognize you, you're the same person who tried to pick my pocket yesterday."

"Goodbye, Senõrita."

The Paseo de La Reforma at midnight was a total drama alone, not to mention Insurgentes Sur or the Avenida Juarez.

Valonga wandered through the streets at midday.

"Bustling" doesn't even come close to describing the motion in this place. There were times when it seemed that the constant motion of the people, the flood of brown-skinned waters threatened to overwhelm her and she would step into a doorway or a cafe, to save herself from the waves.

"Cafe espresso, por favor."

The Cafe Tel Aviv, one of her regular spots. "Nelson Pratt" was beginning to offer her fewer and fewer breaks. "Pratt" had quickly acquired a life of his own. She didn't feel that she was writing any more, "Nelson Pratt" was writing itself.

"Awright now, Valonga, be careful. Sometimes a character can become so strong, he or she will take over and hang you out to dry. Be careful."

She made a mental note to drop Brother O. a letter, to bring him up to date on the book and life in general.

"Are you an American?"

She was tired of trying to explain that she wasn't an American.

"The people who were in America, or whatever they called it, were/are Americans.

My people were imports. We/I am an African-American,

108

nervous, decided to kick it off with a question.

"Why was Bob so surprised that you were having something to eat?"

The eyes glistened, a smile played on Jeangy's mouth.

"Because I haven't eaten anything this year."

"You mean, you haven't had anything in his restaurant?"

"No, I mean that I haven't had anything to eat this year. Anywhere."

Valonga allowed her focus to wander; what was this one bringing her, what was the purpose for her knowing about this scene, this woman?

"A year? You must be a bit snackish by now, aren't you?"

She had tried to make the question a serious one, but it came off sounding frivolous anyway.

"No, I'm not, really. When you draw your nutrition directly from the sun, you're never hungry."

Valonga spaced back a few years, to a book she had read about a famous yogini who had lived on the sun's rays.

"I dine on the sun."

She felt her consciousness floating back to Malana, the braider; "You can get what you wish, if the vibe is right."

"I think I understand what you're saying."

"Of course you do."

They sat, side by side, sipping water, for twenty minutes, patiently waiting for O'toto to serve them his designer dinner.

"Here you are, my queens!" he suddenly announced, and slid two plates in front of them. Jeangy acknowledged his gracious service with an enigmatic smile. Valonga stared at the two African shaped pieces of tofu on her plate, surrounded by gorgeously arranged patterns of shrimp and breaded okra. The design was lovely, like a wonderful painting.

"Bon appetit!" O'toto sang out, and skipped away to lead a wandering couple to a table.

113

"What were you expecting?"

Valonga stared at the translucent orbs of Jeangy's eyes, no longer freaked out by her eye color changes.

"Nothing quite so beautiful as this. Now then, you were telling me about eating the sun?"

"Ahhhhhh yes, the sun."

Valonga forked several morsels of the delicious food into her mouth, pretended not to notice that Jeangy was levitating.

She was clearly sitting on five or six inches of air.

Valonga chewed a piece of shrimp thoughtfully before asking her questions.

"Please, tell me. Who are you?"

Jeangy settled down gently into place, her expression warmed by an inner fire.

' Valonga, I am Jeangy, I'm a space traveler, and I'm here to provide you with some vital information."

Valonga resisted the urge to jump up and run out of the restaurant. O'toto popped up on cue.

"How is it?" he asked solemnly.

"Deep," Valonga responded, not particularly focusing on the food.

O'toto winked at Jeangy and danced away to deal with other matters.

Two more forks of tofu and shrimp and she felt completely satisfied.

"You say you're a space traveler and you're here to provide me with some vital information?"

Jeangy levitated a few inches before answering.

"Yes."

Chapter 11

Valonga strolled up one side of the Paseo de la Reforma and down the other side, her head spinning from the information Jeangy, the space traveler, had laid on her.

"Jeangy, please, before you tell me anything, please tell me what a space traveler is?"

She had stared into her eyes for a full five minutes, seeming to face-read her mind before answering.

"Valonga, a space traveler is one who travels in space. That's the simplest explanation I can give you."

"But how?! I mean...you're not an alien, or anything are you?"

"No, I'm not an alien or anything. I'm a flesh and blood human, just like you."

"Well, how did you become a space traveler? I'm not a space traveler."

"Yes, you are, but you're not traveling from planet to

115

planet, the way I am. You're going from one Master, from one situation to another, and that's what I want to give you information on. Are you ready to receive it?''

Valonga retrieved her key from the flirtatious desk clerk, sprawled out in a chair by the window and stared out at the frenzy of a Mexico City evening.

"Valonga, I have the names of many of the people that you will never meet during this trip you are making, and what could've happened.''

Jeangy, the space traveler, had spoken in a soft, hypnotic voice, her eyes walled back in their sockets. The restaurant filled up with patrons, but they made no sounds. They were the only two people in the world.

"I must make you understand that the people I'm going to talk to you about are just as important, just as real as the people you've met thus far.''

Valonga undressed, pulled on a terry cloth robe and poured herself three fingers of Cuervo Gold, a present from the hotel.

"I'm going to start with Alex Spencer, the nutritionist. I think it's quite appropriate that Alex should be the first person for me to speak of, considering the fact that this conversation is taking place in a restaurant.''

Alex Spenser had given her secret recipes, items of nutrition to prevent aging, cause health problems to disappear and promote a greater union with nature. Or, would have, had they met.

"Use wheatgrass more.''

"Bossmaster Goodwrench, the Jamaican mechanic could *Listen* to a motor and tell you what was the problem.

The problem with him is that he couldn't stop drinking his favorite Jamaican rum.

"Why should I stop drinkin' this rom, mon, it was made with my taste buds in mind.''

116

"Bossmaster fought off success tenaciously, created complex situations out of simple events, was aggressive, ill-tempered, touched to the core by sunsets, beautiful women and well-designed cars. He made life miserable, for himself primarily.

"How would you have met him? Well, your car broke down on a lonely back country road."

Valonga sipped her tequila, trying to follow individual ants in the dusky twilight on the Paseo.

"Charlie Miles had a great deal in common with Bossmaster Goodwrench. First off, they were both quite self-destructive. Goodwrench, the mechanic, the rum lover, and Charlie Miles, the trumpet player's trumpet player hyphen wine, women, heroin, cocaine..."

Charlie, like Goodwrench, had a deep sense of inferiority about what he did. He often spoke in his raspy voice about how society looks at musicians (Goodwrench talked about mechanics). "How would you feel if somebody was telling you: 'get your ass on stage, it's 9 p.m.' like you were a fucking trained seal or some shit!"

Valonga caught the eye of a man strolling on the opposite side of the street. She always seemed to be catching some man's eye.

"And, yes, Valonga, Charlie did make a move on you because Charlie always made a move on an attractive woman."

"You know something, Valonga, I guess you was just one o' them bitches I wasn't supposed to have."

"And, of course, you politely informed him that you weren't a 'bitch.' Or you would have, if it had come to that."

The man, a flirtatious mestizo, paused in a doorway and stared up into the window at her. She sipped her drink and stared back, neutrally.

"Maybe Jesse Jones needed you as much as you needed

117

him. In any case, his staff felt that he needed a stress management consultant on their leader's campaign train. They asked you to keep a low profile because the 'enemy' (anyone not for Jones) was dying to point a malignant finger at the brother's program. In other words, they wanted to say that the brother was crazy for wanting to be President of the United States.''

"And how did it work out, I mean, what happened?''

"Well, number one, your political consciousness was raised a few notches.''

The man puckered his lips, winked, blew her a suave kiss and strolled onward. Probably on his way home to a wife and four kids.

The time at O'toto's with Jeangy, the ambience of the scene washed over her, thoughts about the people Jeangy had talked about, the people she would never meet, made her feel sad.

They were always asking: "What does Jesse want?" It seemed to be such a strange question, 'specially after he had patiently explained a few hundred times—"I want to be the president of the United States.''

"How did I help him?''

"In several important ways; you would've helped him understand himself more completely. You were instrumental in killing off the stereotype that Black men, African-American men, can't be national leaders. You helped him counterattack the racist element quite effectively.''

"I did?''

"I'll say you did. Well, you would have.''

Valonga paced around her room, feeling unfocused, strange. Who am I? Who was that woman?

The notebook called to her. "A Day and Night in the Life of Nelson Pratt.'' She poured another shot of the Gold and settled down at her writing desk. This is something that I feel that I'm on top of.

The restaurant was called Cuisine Internationale and it was owned by a dark skinned man with Japanese eyes. His name is Robert O'toto.

"Berry sorry, Senōra, as you can see we are a store that deals in the arts of Mexico. We have beautiful hand-woven blankets, rebozos, pottery, jewelry. Are you interested in...?"

"There's something wrong here. You don't understand. I was here, in this place, yesterday. I ate dinner in a restaurant here."

"Mexico City is a city with many streets, Senōra; are you certain that the restaurant was on this street?"

Valonga stood in front of "artes de Mexico," staring at the huge sign above the store windows and at the establishments to the right and left of "Artes de Mexico."

This is the place, this was Restaurant Cuisine Internationale yesterday. It was almost like being a part of one of the scenes Jeangy talked about.

"Valonga, you must, sometimes, look at life from the perspective of what might've happened."

She walked quickly back to her hotel to pack. It was time to leave Mexico City.

Nigeria, West Africa. Valonga was on her final leg, this was the home she felt about in her heart, in her soul. It was hot and humid and the smells of lagos permeated the interior of her taxi.

"What's going on? Is there a holiday or something?"

The driver smiled up at her in his rearview mirror.

"No holiday, just lagos in the evening time."

She returned his smile. The whole scene seemed vaguely familiar. There was the Mexico City bustle and hustle with a difference; more color, a richer rhythm.

Rhythm. Rhythm was everywhere. The blaring music

spilling out of shops along the way, the distant sound of drums, the car horns, the rhythms of the voices in the street.

"Here you are, Lady, the Hotel Lagos."

The Hotel Lagos had been recommended to her by a friend back in Augusta, Georgia.

"If you really want to get into what Africa is about, what Nigeria is about, on one level, spend your first night at the Hotel Lagos..."

Valonga struggled with her heavy valises. She traveled lightly, but well.

"You have a reservation for Valonga Prince."

She said it as a statement of fact, the desk clerk made a sly study of her face, her clothes, her luggage, and casually checked the register.

"I'm afraid we are not able to accommodate you, we are all filled up."

She folded the bill and placed it in his crusty right hand. He announced, without hesitation.

"You have room 301."

"Will you have someone bring my bags, please?"

"Yes, of course."

The desk clerk clapped his hands twice and a small, wiry man popped out of a side room. He had obviously been taking a nap.

"Room 301!" the desk clerk barked at the porter.

Valonga felt like helping the little guy struggle up the three flights of stairs with her bags. The elevator entrance wore a yellowed sigh: 'out of order."

The porter hemmed 'n hawwed around until she placed a bill in his hand.

"Thank you. And what is your name?"

The man looked startled, pleased and surprised simultaneously.

"I am called Quickly."

Valonga felt the temptation to laugh. And African-Americans think they've been misnamed.

"Is that your real name?"

"Yes, Quickly Nwabusu."

They smiled into each others face for a moment and then he bowed out of her hotel room, kissing the money she had given him.

Another hotel room. This one was dingier than most of the ones she had occupied during the course of her three year trip to deal with Masters, funkier.

There was no need to unpack. I'm only going to be here one night and after that, Ile Ife was going to be her base for three months, there was no problem in finding it, it was always there. The problem would be to locate Felasha Olatunji.

Felasha Olatunji, master drummer, big time show biz figure.

"I am Felasha Olatunji and all wrongdoers have great reason to fear me because I will tell the truth. I will sing the truth."

Another hotel room, another window.

It all seemed to be chaos, at first, 'til she managed to isolate various happenings.

The heavy set sister, peddling pastry of some kind from a headheld tray, also seemed to be distributing packets of something else. Dope?

The possibility of someone selling dope on a street corner in Lagos, Nigeria, seemed totally out of sync with what she secretly admitted to be a stereotype.

Africa, Nigeria, was supposed to be drums, people doing holistic stuff, not selling drugs on street corners; that was New York, Chicago, Detroit, Watts...

A few more minutes of objective observation affirmed that the sister peddling the pastry from the tray on her head was

121

also peddling small packet of something else.

What the hell is she selling?

Ten minutes later, driven by curiosity, Valonga stepped out onto the street paralleling her hotel. The street seemed so familiar. It could've been Omolu Street in Bahia, or 9th Street, August, Georgia.

The lady selling the pastry from her head tray and the packets from a hidden apron pocket was gone, no where to be seen.

She strolled up one side of the street and down the other side, checking stuff out, being alert, interested, curious.

No, this isn't as foreign as some people wanted to make me think. It seemed so familiar. It could've been Omolu Street or 9th Street, with a couple subtle differences. People were more out. They were living, buying, selling, being on the street, and it didn't seem unusual.

She was instantly spotted as a stranger, but not assaulted because of that fact, either commercially or physically. Her friend in Augusta had given her the right info. The Hotel Lagos was where it was at, to coin a cliche.

Later, in her hotel room, after a dinner reeking with palm oil and delicious flavors, she sprawled out on her lumpy bed, trying to concentrate on "Nelson Pratt," and deal with a serious case of horniness.

She washed her body in the washbasin ("No shower—out of order"), pulled her terry cloth robe on, struck a stirrup-position on the bed and began to masturbate.

The sounds and lights from the streets drifted up as the faces and names of past lovers faded in...

Dave Fry, the fifteen year old "ladies man"...

"I love you, Valonga."

"Dave, we're only fifteen years old, what do we know about love?"

"I know enough to know that I love you."

"Having sex with me doesn't mean that you love me."

Fred, Herbert, John, Amos, Paco, Maurice from Tunisia; she felt the familiar warmth spread from her loins to her shoulder blades, as though an internal steam bath was being slowly turned up to high.

Juan Diablo...the name, the memory pushed her to the physical and emotional peak she need for her orgasm.

Afterwards, she made a ritual of washing herself and pulled out her notebook; "A Day and Night in the Life of Nelson Pratt" was calling.

She assembled her tools, the notebook, a couple ballpoints and the pint of Arc d'triomph cognac she had been saving since she had left Mexico City.

She sat in the low-limbed chair beside her lumpy bed and stared at the wall in front of her. The tears sliding down her cheeks surprised her.

What the hell am I crying about?

She sorted through her feelings, trying to isolate the source of her tears.

God, I'm in Africa, the place where my Ancestors came from. She couldn't isolate the reason for her tears.

Am I happy, sad, what?

There were times in Brazil, in Bahia, when a kind of sadness gripped her. It had to do with knowing that the African people there, like the African people in Georgia, New York, Puerto Rico, Cuba, South Dakota, had been imported, like sardines.

The tears flowed, a strange kind of crying that she felt no control over, an African-American tear jag in Nigeria.

She tried to ignore the tears and began to write, glancing at her outline for directions, from time to time.

"Today is the 23rd of January, 1992 and I am still locked up, doing hard time for a crime I willingly admit to; I was

123

too conscious, too lucid, too clear about what had to be done *not* be imprisoned.

"I was the one who could clearly explain why African-Americans shouldn't start waving the red, white, and blue flag of the oppressor, if there was an opportunity to fly the red, black, and green flag of our aspirations.

"This consciousness, flushed out of me with an eloquence that seemed to flow from a part of my psyche that I couldn't identify, caused me to speak my mind.

"I was too clear about what had to be done to free African-Americans in North and South America. I took the final leap and wrote books about, to, and for my people.

"I think that that was the thing that did it, me writing to my people in a way that only they could understand.

"Yes, I'm 99 percent certain that that was the final straw.

"After all, we weren't supposed to be readers, simply consumers.

"I pissed the dividers and conquerors off by pointing out certain, seemingly obvious circumstances. If entrepreneurs were going to be given an opportunity to make money in our neighborhoods, then we should have, at least, equal opportunities to exploit their neighborhoods. If anyone wanted to do business with us, we should, at least, have the opportunity to do business with them.

"I spoke about this and wrote about it, in a way that was non-racial, and completely comprehensible. The notion of using our people as a dumping ground for all kinds of societal trash bothered me, as it has bothered every sensitive person in this country, for centuries.

"The solution I suggested was simple and unique; we should police our own, with our own police. That didn't go down all with those who have traditionally used their police forces to funnel vices into our communities, and then arrest the people who fall into their traps. I was accused of promoting segregation, preaching self-aid and independence. The attitude of the dominant culture demanded my death and, if my community (and the communities that shared my community's concerns) hadn't threatened to burn America up, they would've killed me.

"They couldn't kill me, they didn't kill me. They locked me up for life and today—January 23rd, 1992—I have been held captive for twenty years.

"They've held me captive for twenty years but my mind remains as free as it ever was."

The sounds of people making sounds, the crowing of roosters and the barking of stray dogs woke her up, the machinery kicked in moments later.

Africa...Africa...Africa...

It was time to move on to Ile Ife ("the house of Ife").

The same desk clerk greeted her, "good morning, I hope you had a good night?"

What did the guy do in his spare time, stay behind the desk day and night?

"I want to go to Ile Ife, can you make arrangements?"

A sly looked curled up the corners of his mouth.

"Yes, my sister, I think it can be arranged."

The sly look gave into a full-fledged malicious smile. Valonga stared at him as though she had no idea what he wanted.

What the hell, let him ask for it.

"Yes, I think it can be arranged, for a price."

"I wasn't under any illusion that I was going to be given a free trip anywhere."

The desk clerk's malicious smile elevated to a grin.

"It will cost you, but it can be arranged. When would you like to leave?"

"This afternoon, if possible. How much will it cost?"

The price he quoted seemed to be a bit much, even for her uneducated bargaining sense. She cut back into him for half the figure he quoted. The grin slipped back to a malicious smile, and finally to the sly look again. They finally haggled down to a price that she felt comfortable with.

"I'd like to leave at 12 noon."

"No problem, no problem."

Valonga stared at the 1980 Chevy as it limped to a stop in front of the Hotel Lagos. There was no mechanical indication that the car would make it to the next block, let alone go up country over rough roads. The desk clerk left his place behind the flyspecked registration desk to stand behind her.

"Ahh hah, I see the car has arrived."

She chilled out the impulse to turn and punch his face. It was 3:30 p.m., she was already worn out from waiting for transportation and now this...clown seemed to be making fun of the whole thing.

"Don't you think you're being very generous to call this piece of shit a car?."

The desk clerk accepted her anger gracefully.

"It is a wonderful car, you will have no trouble getting to Ile Ife."

"I can't believe you, but that's beside the point. What took so long for it to get here?"

"My uncle had to do some business and I could not have the use of it 'til now."

Valonga was startled to see Quickly Nwabusu bump open the door of the Chevy and struggle to put her bags in the back seat of the car.

"You're the driver?"

"Yes, I am your driver," he replied and doffed his Phillip Morris pillbox hat politely.

There was nothing to do but flow with the flow. She had

learned that as a part of her stress management training, and
honed it to a fine edge in Brazil, Cuba, Spain and Mexico.

"Why Ile Ife?" the desk clerk had asked as she counted
out the required number of nairas into his greedy hands.

"Because I'm told it's the Bahia of Nigeria, and that's
where I want to be, in the soul."

Three hours later they were on the outskirts of Lagos.

"We are beyond most of the madness now, Miss Balongo.
There is only the insanity of the road ahead of us."

Valonga smiled across at her driver, hoping that her smile
wasn't a caricature of the desk clerk's malicious grin. The
trip through the streets and on the freeways was something
she promised herself she would never forget.

The Nigerian drivers seemed to be gripped by suicidal
tendencies. She had never experienced such total disregard
for the rules, not even in Mexico.

"Quickly, do people drive this strangely all the time?"

"It used to be worse."

She grew to like Quickly Nwabusu, quickly. They were
suddenly thrown into the eye of a storm (Lagos, Nigeria,
traffic) and forced to become instant fatalists together.

Quickly drove the Chevy with a minimum amount of
concentration, humming secret little tunes to himself in
between the occasional questions Valonga put to him.

"Where are you from, Quickly?"

"I am from the east, M'am, from the east."

The car ran surprisingly well, when it was running.

"Quickly, why are we stopping, are we out of gas?"

"No, Miss Balongo, we are not out of gas. I am stopping
to give the car a chance to rest."

Valonga made a quick, careful reading of the man's
profile, to try to determine if he was pulling her leg.

He wasn't pulling her leg, he was serious. They paused

on a rutted road near a village, she could see and hear the sounds.

Quickly motioned for her to get out of the car. He opened the hood and spoke to the engine. She stood off to his left, taking in the scene. They were in the 20th century, on a road that she hoped would take her to her destination and the man driving her there had to stop "to rest" the car.

"Was Ogun pleased with your prayer?"

He didn't seem surprised that she knew what he was doing.

"Well, so far so good."

He almost made her laugh aloud. He was such a dry little guy, no fat about him anywhere, not even in his speech.

The night air washing her face was refreshing, and, at the same time, vaguely threatening. During the course of one smooth stretch of road she had the feeling that a soft hand was caressing both her cheeks.

"Quickly, I can drive a bit if you feel tired."

The man immediately slowed to a stop in the middle of the road, opened his door, came around to her side, gestured for her to take the wheel.

He climbed into the back seat with her bags.

"Tell me please when we reach Ibadan."

Valonga took the wheel and accelerated to a fast forty miles per hour. She had been watching Quickly drive and knew that it wasn't safe to go beyond that speed.

A stray goat wandered across the road. A flock of vultures flew up from the 9 p.m. meal in the center of the road.

What was it? A man? An animal?

Afrika, a woman with a baby on her back, squatted on the shoulder of the road. Afrika, a large man dressed in colorful robes standing on the shoulder of the road, calmly smoking a pipe. Was he waiting for somebody?

The potholes, the uneven surface of the roadway caused her a few problems at first, but then she learned to relax, to give the car it's head, in a manner of speaking. The sudden staccato of drums startled her. They seemed very close and far away at the same time. She pulled the car over to the side of the road.

"Are we in Ibadan, Miss Balongo?"

"No, not yet. I'm just giving the car a chance to rest."

Quickly smiled without opening his eyes and snored on.

Valonga stepped out of the car into the darkness. She could see millions of stars and the light of a distant fire off to her left. I wish there was somebody here that I was in love with, that I could share this with...

Ibadan made her feel as though she had stepped through a time warp, into the 15th century. Or maybe the 18th century.

They arrived on a market day, dawn in Ibadan.

"Quickly, this is Ibadan."

The wiry chauffeur/porter/man about Nigeria, yawned himself awake, took the wheel and drove straight through Ibadan.

"That was Ibadan," he announced, twenty miles northeast of the city.

"So, I gathered."

Quickly Nwabusu walked inside the Ile Ife version of the Hotel Lagos.

"This is a good place to stay in Ile Ife."

She felt no need to question his judgment. The place couldn't be any worse than the Hotel Lagos.

Her plan was to rent a house and become a part of the scene, finish her novel and return to Augusta, Georgia (and the business of stress management) via Bahia, Brazil.

It was 11:30 p.m. and she could feel Ile Ife throbbing in the night.

"Quickly, are you returning to Lagos tonight?"

129

"Yes, Miss Balonga, I must return as quickly as possible, I will sleep on the way."

"Not while you're driving, I hope."

"No, Miss Balonga, I will pause the car beside the road and sleep."

She sprawled on the bed, a damp towel on her forehead, her attention drawn to the old-fashioned propeller fan going around in the ceiling. It moved too slowly to cool her off, but the motion was hypnotic. The staccato thumping of drums woke her up. They carried the same rhythms she had heard on the road. She felt disoriented for a few moments. How could the drummers she had heard on the road be the same as the ones she heard now?

Memories of her time with Armando Bá floated in on her.

"There are rhythms, Balonga, rhythms that speak to us of the here and the there. Dig me?"

Rhythms, compelling urges forced her to pull her notebook into bed with her, below the hypnotically twirling fan.

"A Day and a Night in the Life of Nelson Pratt" was calling; he wanted to talk about the war that Iraq pulled in on itself.

"August 2, 1990, the Iraqi ruler, Saddam Hussein, invaded Kuwait, setting off chain reactions that will never stop. The United States immediately pressed the United Nations into service on it's behalf (and pressured the Saudi Arabians into allowing a coalition of oil hungry nations to send sorties from it's land).

"Reagan (alias, to the cognoscenti, as "Ray-gun"), had tried desperately to get the country into a central American war, but failed, had bequested his legacy to Bush, the ex-CIA headman.

"The United States made it clear to Hussein (via their ambassadors in Iraq) that they wouldn't interfere with a little landgrabbing (Connie Chung got the whole story 2/11/91 on "Face to Face," an interview that showed the ambassadress in a session with Saddam Hussein, explaining exactly that).

"The U.S. government lied, of course, and when the dictator of Iraq crossed into Kuwait, the U.S. had it's reason for getting into the Gulf.

"It was a masterful piece of business, worthy of the best written scenarios of this century.

"The United States (a government that supported Somoza, Trujillo, Papa Dock, killed Allende, destabilized Guatemala, turned Mexico into a satellite, propped apartheid up, supplied arms to just about every fascist government in the world, jumped on Grenada, Panama, with all four feet, kept hands off the Russia's crushing of Afghanistan, Latvia, Estonia, Lithuania, used the World Bank like a pawnshop (Brazil), tried to destroy Vietnam, made genocide of the native Americans, a national policy until late into the 20th century, and tried to keep the Africans imported to America in a state of perpetual servitude, practically forced Saudi Arabia into accepting "help").

"Suddenly the United States was concerned about Saddam Hussein's take over of Kuwait (some suggest that the rich reserves of Kuwaiti oil had something to do with it) and got busy.

"Saddam Hussein had made a mistake and the U.S. was going to make him pay for it. 500,000 men and women (professional soldiers, mercenaries) were sent to the desert. Desert Shield soon became Desert Storm, the "war" was on.

"The United States was basking in blood; it had a "stubborn" enemy and new weapons to test. The Air Force took the point...

"Bush and buddies didn't miss a public relations trick.

"They were not going to repeat the Vietnam—bodybag—war on dinnertime TV again. This was going to be a clean-cut Nintendo baby. And it *was* up 'til the Iraqi leader scud-bombed Tel Aviv.

"The United States persuaded the Israelis to be cool, for the sake of maintaining a coalition that included Syrians and Egyptians. And that they would get some money later.

"'Don't worry, we'll Patriot those babies out of the sky for you.'

"Weeks into the bombing raids on Baghdad and Basra, after oil pollution had damaged a sector of the gulf beyond repair, the ground repair, the ground troops were set loose.

"America waved more flags and tied more yellow ribbons around more posts than ever before in history, we were not going to feel the guilt we felt during and after Vietnam.

"The biggest lies were the best.

"We're over there to restore democracy to Kuwait."

"'We've got to stop Saddam Hussein before he invades Spain.'

"'If we don't stop him now, we won't be able to stop him.'

"The president who vetoed the Civil Rights Bill of 1990 had a professional army that was disproportionately composed of semi-citizens (African-Americans). Many of them were semi-crazed by the hypocritical vice they were squeezed into.

"'Sure, we're gonna fight, what choice do we have, we volunteered for this bullshit.'

"The shit hit the fan when the troops hit the beaches of Kuwait."

The persistent drumming finally forced her to stop writing. She felt at ease with a community where no one yelled out of a window, "stop making all that noise!"

She was in Nigeria, West Africa, and the persistent drumming seemed natural, a part of the scene.

Whatever they're drumming for is intense, I can feel that.

132

She nodded off under the hypnotically circling fan, her thoughts on America after the Persian Gulf war and the prospect of finding a house to live in, in Ile Ife.

Chapter 12

After a week she felt as though she had been living in Ile Ife for years. The people were reserved, but not snobbish or aloof, once they felt the ice had been broken.

Valonga worked out a routine for herself, after she had managed to find a hip little two bedroom house on the edge of town.

"We have rented this house before, to other Black Americans like yourself."

She didn't find out who the other African-Americans had been, but they had evidently left a reservoir of good will behind.

"They stayed here for a year, a woman in a wheelchair, with a son and her friend, who had two daughters and a son."

Up early for an hour of Capoeira Angola before the heat and humidity settled in. The exercise period attracted neighborhood boys and girls, who squatted at the perimeters of her yard, exchanging solemn remarks and expression.

Off to the market after a quick swab off, home for brunch. Back to "Nelson Pratt." Something in town, a performance, or just simple strolling everywhere before dinner and/or more writing. There was a lot to experience.

She felt loose and free in Ile Ife, apart from the people, but *connected*. They smiled to each other and exchanged greetings and, after a month, began to close in on each other.

Visitors showed up, neighbors and people like Dr. John Henry Ivan Hope, a world famous Ourstorian. She felt honored to receive the man who had written "Stolen Souls."

"How do you do, my name is John Henry Ivan Hope and I'm a Ourstorian."

Dr. Hopoe was in his 90's, partially blind, filled with knowledge about Africa, Africans and Africans in the Diaspora.

"No, no, I don't feel the least bit put out because I haven't been "validated" by the so-called "mainstream" historians."

He was a totally gracious man.

"When they told me that a young Black woman, from America was staying here I felt compelled to pay you a visit."

He stayed for a precious few days, she tried to encourage him to stay longer.

"Dr. Hope, I have everything you need here, and whatever I don't have that you need, I can get."

"I appreciate what you're saying but I believe, as the old saying goes, that guests and fish stink after three days."

He left her with hundreds of new ideas and concepts.

"Africans were great explores, but not great conquerors. For example, African explorers made many trips to what we now call America, but they didn't consider "conquering" it, that's a perverted Eurocentric concept."

Why is it a Eurocentric concept? I have theories but I can't

136

say that I *know*. Perhaps the European psyche, re-cycled through the provincialism that comes from being hemmed in by narrow boundaries, was stabbing in the collective racial psyche for a way out. Who knows?

In any case, the horrors that the colored people of the world have suffered from this malevolence is immeasurable.

"Of course, yes, of course, humanity had it's beginning on the African continent, but the Eurocentric idiots have tried to deny that fact since the first His-story was printed."

"And, yes, once again, of course, we had African astronauts; way back in ancient times, but it was such an ordinary thing that people didn't even trip on it, as you young people used to say. I have spoken with some of the Dogon elders who remember the names of their astronauts. This is confidential information, you understand, and they don't pass it around like Kleenex tissues."

She felt a sense of loss after his departure, as though a library had been closed for the rest of the semester. That's one of the proverbs that they say; "when an Elder dies, a building filled with knowledge has been burned."

Sugah Baby came. Sugah Baby Ali, the Boxer.

"I am the greatest that ever was!"

"What're you doing in Ile Ife, in Nigeria, West Africa?"

"Hey, looka here, sisterwoman, I am an African man, O.K.? And what I felt compelled to do was show my stuff to the sister...and the brothers over here on the continent, O.K.?"

He was the most egotistical man she had ever met and also, one of the nicest.

"How they treatin' you over here in the jungle, anybody buggin' you."

He set up a training camp for two weeks in an unused soccer stadium, a half mile from her house. He was a fitness freak who tripped on the fact that she would join him for a five mile run at 7:30 a.m. Capoeira Angola...

"Wowwwww! This shit is the max, O.K.?"

He missed the subtle flavors of the art, but clearly understood what the purpose of the business was about.

"You know something?!" You could kill a motherfucker with some shit like this."

He insisted that his name be misspelled: "Sugah."

"I honor the memory of the immortal Sugar Ray Robinson, I am not he. I honor the memory of the great Sugar Ray Robinson, I am not he. I *am* Sugah Baby Ali, and I am a whole new ballgame. I'm something else."

After a couple weeks she felt that she was breaking through his egotistical crust, a part of his self defense system.

"Sugah, I'm writing a story about boxing, tell me what goes through your head when you prepare for a fight."

He blinked with surprise and splattered a buzzing fly to death.

"What do I think? I think about how much trouble the poor rascal is in, picking a fight with me."

"Well, I mean, beyond that, deeper than that."

He didn't blink again and when he answered her, his voice conveyed a melancholic streak she had never heard before.

"It's deep, sister, really deep, and I'm not sure I can really explain it."

They were sitting on the back porch of her house, sipping glasses of lemonade, casually watching her neighbors watch them.

"It's like how you describe writing to be, O.K.?"

She nodded, shades of Brother O.

"O.K.?"

She nodded once again, Sugah Baby needed lots of affirmation.

"Number one, this whole thing is on you until you get into the ring with your opponent. See how that works?"

She nodded quickly.

"I mean, you can't be any better than you think you are, O.K.? You run and punch and do situps and the whole bunch of other physical stuff, O.K.? And they got people around you all the time.

"Your sparring mates, your trainer, people coming to the camp for different reasons, O.K.? Your attorney, your tax guide, your p.r. man, if you wanna go that route.

"All of this stuff is taking place in the open, up front for everybody to see, O.K.? But the other side of it, the deep-inner side of it is locked in where nobody can see it."

Valonga reacted with a quiet show of surprise to see the sudden, fearful look glaze over Sugah baby's face.

"Yeahhh, that's where it really is, O.K.? All up inside yourself. You know that when all the situps have been done, and after all the loud talkin' is over, you gonna gave to pop up in a squared-off ring to get in a fist fight with a man who is just as well prepared as you are, and thinks he's badder than you, O.K.?"

"Does that cause you problems.?"

"Well, it doesn't exactly cause me problems, not yet anyway. But I've studied the films of the old timers—Sugar Ray Robinson, Joe Louis, Walcott, Bratton, Leonard, all of 'em, O.K.? There's that point they get to in their careers when the fear of being beaten begins to eat 'em up.

"I think Muhammed Ali is one of the very few who didn't show the fear. It's a good thing he got out when he did."

She thought back to all the Muhammed Ali fights she'd watched with her father. Two days later Sugah Baby Ali was back on the road...

She missed him instantly, but the slack was immediately taken up by "Nelson Pratt."

"Bush had lots of new technology to play with, and a

perfect stage to play his play on. Saddam Hussein was a really naughty boy and the p.r. campaign that was waged was incredible.

"The ground war in the desert started off with few casualties and lots of prisoners. I felt offended, violated in some ways, by the general American attitude toward the African-American men and women in the Gulf. Or maybe we should blame it on the media. Despite the fact that it was generally acknowledged that a disproportionate number of the troops were African-Americans (something like 25%, out of an African-American population of 12%), they didn't seem to exist.

"Colin Powell, the African-American head of Operation Desert Storm and the Joint Chiefs of Staff, never really counted as an African-American person, in my book. He had reached the point in his psyche where he was simply a professional soldier doing his duty. Yes, of course, he was identified as a Black man, but in his case it ranked with name, rank, and serial number.

"What I'm trying to say is that I got nothing visceral out of him, no deep feelings that he was telling Bush that he had fucked up with Africans in America by using every available dollar to develop some shit that was not going to ultimately benefit the nation.

"The media ignored the African-Americans in the desert. They put an African face on the screen, from time to time, but it was done as though circumstances forced them to do it. They (the media) interviewed 'Hispanics,' run of the mill white folks, piles of white politicians, but skipped past Maxine Waters and Ron Dellums.

"White men (and women) told us what was going on in the Gulf war. You would've thought, just because there were so many Black men and women fighting over there that the media would've made some effort to reflect that reality. They didn't.

"It was almost as though they took us for granted."

The rain stopped her from exercising outside and from writing for a few days. The rain was lush, sweet smelling, fervent.

She spent hours sitting on the enclosed porch of her house, hypnotized by tropical downpours that seemed capable of washing the world away. She surrendered to the rhythms of the rain, wandered around inside her head, reclaimed the experiences she had had and the ones she was having.

Capoeira Angola always claimed the first part of her heart and her head, Bahia, Brazil. For hours she listened to the rhythms of the Berimbau, the Pandiero, the Reco-Reco, the Agogo, and the Atabaque.

There were times when the slow, regular heartbeat rhythms of the rain forced her to sing songs from the Capoeira Angola tradition that she didn't know she knew.

In Africa, in Nigeria, she felt the pull of this African-based martial art more heavily than she had ever felt it. She felt it's rhythms, pulses, more strongly.

She wanted a man. She wanted a man as a luxury item, she didn't feel that she *needed* one, it wasn't that kind of feeling.

Valonga watched the men passing in the muddy road in front of her house and thought about reeling one of them inside. It would be easy, they all know I'm here and any one of them would love to have sex with me. She felt that sure of herself. As a futuristic thinking, "aggressive-minded" African-American woman from Georgia, who owned a stress management firm, she felt definitely on top of the man-woman stuff in Africa.

Maybe my perspective is warped, maybe I shouldn't think this way. She fasted for seven days, allowing her mind a chance to be clean, to reflect. Drums started sounding on the second day, as she sprawled out on her front room floor and offered thanks to Sango. (Shango).

"Sango, I feel that I know you because...

"I've always loved the sight and sound of thunder and lightning, and I've always thought that liars and thieves should be punished by celestial elements, not anything down here. Maybe this is a kind of specious knowledge, but there it is."

She exercised herself, slowly, with a conscious effort to discover new feelings in the movements. One afternoon, the rain threatening to become a blue fire outside, she turned on a tape by the Mestre Pastinha and discovered elements of the Angola ginga that she had never known.

The Angola ginga, this low down, almost squatting, knees bent position, had struck her as a very awkward position to be in. That is 'til she had seen Mestre Juizo uncoil from it, like a cobra springing from it's curled up position, or a mongoose.

She played through an hour of movements in the low Angola Capoeira ginga, and then collapsed on the kitchen floor, laughing out loud, her thigh muscles screaming. She replayed life through the bullfight with "Machete," sprawled on the floor, her thigh muscles twitching and screaming.

"Valonga, remember this...the faena is where the bull is going to be killed as artistically as possible, or the artist, because the bull, he is a great critic of this activity."

She spent a half day doing full-blooded veronicas with a kente accented cape. The gash in her upper right thigh ached a bit from the dampness.

It wasn't difficult to call up Armando Ba. The village of Boca Grande was Ile Ife on a smaller scale.

"Valonga, the ritmos of Africa are the rhythms of the world. I don' know why this is the case, but this is it, you dig?''

Within the call and response of the rain beats on her roof, there were always the contrapuntal rhythms of the Afro-Cuban master of percussion.

"Some pure stuff was synthesized here, you know what I mean? Who can say? Maybe the slave trade-genocide thing was what the Orisa had designed for us to make this new music. I can't say, O.K.?''

Valonga played on a small wooden box for five hours one day, recalling Armando Ba's advice.

"Do not resist the rhythm—go wid it!''

Master Kimio Eta, under the circumstances, was not much a source of frustration as she had originally thought it to be. The Master knew it wasn't for me. He knew that wasn't in me. She smiled at the memory of Kunzai, the man who had helped her get in to see Master Eta.

"I am English." Meaning, I speak English.

Master Kimio Eta and the koto, a man who related to Ray Charles, but pulled back from the idea of trying to teach her how to play the koto.

Master Kim and the art of Tae Kwon Do intermingled. They had made me understand how clearly the Asian mind was. Either you are it or you're not, and they've had enough experience with westerners aping their activities to know that.

"Hey 'com'on, sister, that's a lot of what writing is about. Magic.''

Brother O., the Thai restaurant, the fried fish, "the things we are destined to do.''

"The war had been fought quickly, savagely, surgically, thousands of Iraqi's died and a few 'coalition' members.

"Bush had promised the 'coalition' everything; Israel was paid not to meddle for a bunch of money, Syria, Egypt, England and all the rest were pulled in by the spoils to be shared. Politics do make strange bed fellows.

"Many Arabs felt that Hussein had broken even because he survived the war.

"It was some crazy shit, a kind of goat going to slaughter thing. Iraqi troops surrendered by the thousands, it was worse than the Italian troop scene in World War II."

The writing grabbed her at different times of the morning, afternoon, evening, but especially at night. It made her feel special, as though she were participating in a ceremony.

Sometimes, when she wrote at night and she could hear drums coming from 'way off, they seemed to be a part of what she was writing.

Her trip fascinated her. Candomble and Capoeira Angola in Brazil, the conga with Armando Ba in Cuba, the opportunity to beg to learn the Koto from Master Eta, Malana, the Braider.

"Valonga, Africa is going to blow your mind."

She wandered out onto the porch and stared into a distance beyond her eyes. The sky glowed with warmth, it enveloped her, made her sprawl out on the porch.

God, it's so beautiful to listen to it rain.

"Be careful, Valonga, you may get what you wish for."

Had the mysterious man on the boat, on the Anabacoa, been real or had she imagined him?

Almost three years of doing what she wanted to do had freed her of a lot of inhibitions.

It's getting to be time for me to share my life with someone, to be wanted forever by the same person. She smiled at how old-fashioned that seemed. But it's really what I want.

Diablo formalized from the misty air on the porch and gently dived on top of her.

"Have you missed me?"

"Yes."

"You thought we would never see each other again?"

"I had considered that."

Her caftan was soaked with the mist, she felt it as a warmer skin. She stood up, swaying to the rhythms she heard from the rain.

Life was so mysterious and beautiful; why don't people allow themselves to trip out more often? They have to get sick and have a life-threatening experience before they can go out there for a break.

She crawled back into the house, feeling at ease on her hands and knees. She wandered into the shabby little closet called a toilet to take a pee, sat there listening to the piss on her roof.

"God pissing through a sieve."

Malana spoke to her: "I think one of the most beautiful things in the world is to have a good woman friend. Men are great, too, but women are like me."

Malana braids life the way she braids hair. Some of her interweaves were too intricate to understand.

"Do they know who I am?"

It was time to go back. "Nelson Pratt" was going to be the beginning of another career. It would help her Capoeira Angola immensely.

"It was over very quickly, less than three months. After the deadline, January 15, had been extended by one day, the American Air Force was unleashed on Iraq, joined with Saudi Arabian, Kuwaiti, British, French, Italians . . .

"The bombing was devastating. Saddam Hussein was on the receiving end of the western world's meanest technology.

"If you lived in America at the time you would've been intensely distressed, or puffed up, depending on your orientation.

"The anti-war movements were muffled and a gigantic

145

guilt/greed trip forced thousands of Americans to tie yellow ribbons around harmless trees and to fling the stars 'n stripes out over every available building. It didn't take a lot of smarts to figure out why so many people had become patriotic all of a sudden.

"Subconsciously, most of the citizens remembered the way the Vietnam vets had been treated. They were obviously determined to let the Gulf War vets know that they were appreciated.

"(The Grenada/Panama guys were/had been part of secret jokes, not to be taken seriously. This was serious, this was about oil. 'Blood for oil.')

"March 3, 1991, in Los Angeles, an African-American man was beaten like a beast without a soul by ten or fifteen white policemen. The scene was captured on video by a white guy from the building across the street.

"Somehow it seemed to fit into the scene just right; African-American men and women were returning from the job of freeing a semi-dictatorship from the grasp of an egomaniac. They had been sent by a President who had vetoed the Civil Rights Bill of 1990, and now, one of their brothers was suffering from the slings and arrows of outrageous police behavior.

"The attack on the man in the street signalled the beginning of a resurgence of African-American militancy.

"In Los Angeles they screamed for the police chief's resignation. The police chief, a racist, had often told the complainers to kiss his ass, more or less.

"In the years that I've spent in this place for unspecified crimes I've watched racism become more sophisticated, more entrenched all the time. It just doesn't seem that America can shake itself free from it's past, or should I be more specific and say that the European-Americans don't seem to be able to shake themselves free of their bullshit."

Chapter 13

It was time to back, to retrace her steps. Georgia seemed closer all the time, watching the Nigerian earth dip off into rivulets. She hadn't been disappointed in Africa, she hadn't yearned for efficient-efficient telephone systems and extra quick sales talks. She hadn't carried a torch for American technology anywhere. But it was time to return to the business, time to give the next deserving member of the business a chance to go out, to milk their dreams.

She strolled to the window to talk to Jeangy, leaning into the half-screened window from the other side.

"So, I see you made it to Africa, huh?"

Valonga settled into a chair beside the window. It all seemed so natural; the fasting, the visits by people she would never have known in Georgia, the impossible rhythms of the rains, Jeangy. Am I hallucinating?

"Yes, I made it to Africa, and in a few weeks I'll be

leaving for Bahia."

"Your timing is excellent."

"Why do you say that?"

A mysterious smile lurked in the corners of Jeangy's mouth for a moment.

"You'll find out."

A solid sheet of rain suddenly replaced the space traveler's image.

On the plane to Germany, two weeks later, Valonga stared at the headlines—"coup in Ile Ife, Nigeria, thousand killed." She folded the newspaper and placed it in the seat next to her.

Mestre Juizo and Capoeira Angola were in exactly the same place they had been in when she left.

"Valonga, you have *not* been doing the movements. I can tell."

She smiled and settled back into the routine of practice, soreness, practice, soreness practice. And for one glorious week, painfree, she played Capoeira Angola as though she was born to do it.

"Valonga, your rastiera is improving..."

"Felasha Kun, 1st time in Brazil, one performance only, September 15th, 1992."

Jeangy was right, the only thing we have to do is relax and everything would come into focus.

"Valonga, who is this man, Kun?"

Felasha Kun, master musician, moral and political conscience of his country, great spirit.

"He was one of the reasons why I made my trip to Nigeria but I could never find him. It's a blessing to be able to see him in Brazil."

September 15th, 1991. Valonga sat bolt upright in her expensive seat. The Brazilians fluttered around her like excited butterflies. They had been waiting for an hour-and-a-half.

Valonga knew from rumor and legend that Felasha Kun was always "Late." She had never heard of him being on "time."

Fifteen minutes later they heard the bottom notes of two talking drums from behind the curtains, and ten minutes later, as though another world was open up, the singers, dancers, drummers and Master Kun filled the stage. The color and pageantry overwhelmed them, the incredible stories of ancient Nigerian, Ghanaiian and Malian Kingdoms told in song and dance.

They moved the audience from village to village, from country to country with talking drums and djimbe, they changed scenes with the ease of a sister switching into another lapa.

Valonga sat and absorbed for three hours, no intermission. And suddenly it was all over, the master musician was easing off stage, singing a poignant song about men who have to see the world in order not to get lost in it.

The audience was stunned into pregnant silence for a moment, and then irrupted with a rush of joyful noise. Some of them danced in the aisles, people chanted: "More Felasha! More Felasha! More Kun! More Kun!"

The chanting went on for a half-hour or more, Valonga wedged her way through the aisle. She had experienced the great Felasha Kun and now she understood something about the sheer magic of feeling that she had never known before.

Felasha Kun had opened up spiritual doors for her, for many people. Maybe I was supposed to see him here, and not in Nigeria. Maybe that's what the spiritual calender opened up to.

She strolled the midnight streets of her sector of Salvador, Bahia, pulling in the fragrant night airs, clearly thinking. I'll be leaving all this in another week. The thought made her feel uneasy, almost sad. Going back home, going back to Georgia.

"It now appears that I'm going to be released from prison, that I will be able to return to the revolutionary life on the outside. All the legal signs are pointing at an exit, but I'm not going to begin cheering until I'm back out there again.

"I've been a captive of the state for twenty-five years. I'm fifty years old now, strong physically and mentally, anxious to get on with the struggle.

"Strangely, to some people, I don't feel bitter or evil and conquered. I feel eager and alert. I feel as though this prison stay has been a footnote in my life, something I could've done without, but there it is, a 'done deal' and I've been dealing with what was done.

"I feel as though I could fight racism for the next one-hundred-thousand years. Racism. It took me ten years to find out what to do with my understanding of it.

"Before I was framed and placed in this place to rot, I'd always thought myself to be a racist. I seemed to have eminent qualifications: I didn't like Europeans in general, and European-Americans specifically. I felt that way until it was fixed in my head that in order to be a racist I would have to have economic control of another race's destiny. And political control.

"Being an African in America has never allowed me to control anybody elses economic destiny, ergo, I could not be a racist.

"The Japanese (in their attitudes toward the Ainu, the Okinawans, the Burakumen, the Hiroshima burnees) can give a perfect demonstration of what racism is.

"It should be declared a mental illness, with schizophrenia, paranoia, and all the rest.

"Some folks will question my suggestion to make it a

150

category of mental illness. Maybe they will see something contradictory in saying that the racist has, or wants to have economic control of another race's economic destiny.

"This great urge to have economic control of another race is the greatest manifestation of the illness. There are also other symptoms that reveal the vicious nature of this aberration.

"Briefly, a few of these symptoms:

A) The racist is oblivious to the suffering and anguish he/she causes. In modern times, the South Afrikan Boer and the crack salesmen are standup examples.

"These are the kinds of people who sell their own children into slavery.

B) The racist is basically a hopeless creature. They have no *basic* belief in the possibility of life existing without hate. They nurture themselves on pessimism.

C) The racist always envies the men of color and wants his woman. If the racist is anti-semitic, for example, he will figure a way to turn the blondest jew into a Sephardic shepherd and his wife into a long suffering Aryan honey cake.

"The man needs killing and the woman needs a 'real man,' so thinks the racist.

D) The racist is able to act inhumanely at any time. That is one of the specific areas to be studied, not nearly enough work has been done on this.

E) And finally (I said, briefly) we have the anti-racist racist, the 'liberals' who reveal a strain of racism that is as difficult to get rid of as Vietnamese claps without penicillin.

"The anti-racist racists are extremely well-armed (with their patronizing attitudes and devotion to the darker races) and maybe considered the most dangerous. It all depends on what time of year you run into them.

"If they've spent the summer in a sunny spot and feel tanned enough, they're apt to begin to believe they're as good as people of color.

"People of color, people with heavy splashes of melanin in their skins. How long is it going to take us to realize that melanin is an energy receiver, a receptor that pulls it's genius straight from the sun's rays?

"Hundreds of melanin researchers have reached the same conclusion, that this pigment enriching substance in responsible for creating superior human beings, and so few people want to go on record, saying, in essence, we are the essence."

The bus trip from Atlanta to Augusta offered her just the right span of time to review and update. She stared at the mint green fields and the brick red dirt fringing the road. Home again.

The business was going well, contradicting the people who had predicted disaster from the moment she decided to establish herself in a middle-sized southern city.

"A stress management firm in Augusta? Who're you going to do business with, all they do is catfish and walk slow."

She mentally organized her next few days; check in with Momma, spend a day "re-orienting," a couple days loafing before going back into the office mode to release the next three year "vacationeer."

Augusta, Georgia, the bus terminal.

She checked her bags into a storage locker and decided to walk around for a bit, to "re-sniff," as her father once put it.

"Nelson Pratt" was finding it's way into the final chapter and the vision of her next subject was beginning to rear it's head in her daydreams.

The humidity of the evening made her think of Bahia. She made a right turn at the end of the block, subconsciously heading for "her side of town." She nodded to the sculptured faces that nodded to her from their trellised porches.

African people everywhere are so warm. We're either loving each other or killing each other.

She exchanged quiet greetings with a Mestre Juizo, waved to Armando Bá driving past, peeked into Master Kim's recently opened Tae Kwon Do studio on 7th Street, and felt the spiritual presence of hundreds of other people she had shared time with during the course of her trip.

Jeangy materialized, strolling up Gwinnett street to Paine College.

"Well, how does it feel to be back home?"

"Hard to say, I just got here."

Jeangy matched her slow stroll for a half block and left her.

"Talk to you later, Valonga, I have some urgent interplanetary business to deal with."

"See you later, Jeangy."

She watched the space disassemble, evaporate.

The Paine College campus was settling into the after dinner-study time. Valonga settled into the full lotus position at the foot of the largest tree on campus. The soft buzzing of a million insects and the cool of the evening shadows lulled her into a dreamy state.

She was on the riverbank with Malana, the Braider, again. She felt beautiful, lovely, sensual, gorgeous.

Large and small birds, fantastically feathered, fluttered onto the trees near her. She felt the presence of the man, sensitive, honest, and loving.

The man cradled Valonga in his arms, kissed her as though he was sipping nectar from a flower. They caressed each other. Once again, she was woman and he was man and no one needed to ask questions.

After hours of slow motion love, the man stood and backed away from her, smiling beautifully, leaving her with another perfect memory. She didn't feel the urge to know him beyond where they had been together. It had been perfect and she felt no need to spoil it with any emotional pressures beyond the ones they had shared.

Malana's image drifted from the lower branches of the tree, cautioned her: "Remember, Valonga, you can get what you wish if the vibe is right."

The rhythms of Capoeira Angola stirred her to another level of consciousness. She slowly opened her eyes, her ears catching the music of a distant berimbau.

She stood and started swaying to the elegant sounds of the Capoeira Angola rhythm. A step forward, a half step backward, a quick knee dip, a cobra-like kick to the invisible groin.

She stopped her ginga after a few minutes, bathed by the lingering humidity. What sense does it make to come back to any of this when my heart belongs to Bahia?

She stared into the heavens, tracing star patterns, and started the long walk back to the bus station.

Her thighs felt tight after the ginga and she laughed aloud, visualizing the welcome she would receive when she returned to Mestre Juizo's academy.

Of course, that's where I belong. Isn't that what the Mae de Santos predicted for me?

"Eventually you must return to Candomblé, you understand?"

And after I return, she questioned herself, then what?

Brother O.'s brassy baritone echoed in the back of her mind—"Write about it, dammit! Write about it!"

END

Candomblé—(def./explanation) One of the African religions of Brazil.

Epilogue/Valonga

The ocean breezes swept across the slack bodies laced across the beach, gently drifted through the narrow streets and plazas of the city, awakening those who were asleep, strengthening those who were having their second cup of café of the morning.

It was the final day and night of the carnival and special events were planned for the whole time frame. The big event for Valonga was the Capoeira Angola roda scheduled for midday in the Plaza Pelourinho, the place where rebellious slaves were once publicly whipped for their reluctance to serve faithfully.

Valonga stirred slowly in her bed, cautiously moving one leg to the edge of the bed, followed by the other one.

"Ohhhhhh..."

The involuntary moan startled her for a moment, made her feel that someone else was making the sound.

Oh my poor body. She pulled herself into a sitting position on the side of the bed, perspiration soaking her back and forehead with the effort.

"Ohhhhhh..."

She slumped on the side of the bed, trying to figure out how she was going to get to the toilet across the room. I feel like a whipped snake.

The urge to urinate finally forced her to stand and begin the painful trek to the toilet. Minutes later she lowered herself to the toilet seat.

"Ohhhhhh..."

She was sore from her neck down to her ankles. Incredible. How can I feel this sore and stiff after all these months?

She replayed her mental tape for a few minutes, trying to isolate the answer. Carnival, that's it. She smiled at her deduction as though someone had told her a bad joke. Carnival, that's it.

A hard practice session under Mestre Juizo, yesterday.

"Valonga, pay attenshun! You are dreaming of something that is not here!"

A beautiful roda after the practice session was over, all thirty students playing Capoeira Angola with each other once or twice. She straightened her back slightly.

She had even had the opportunity to play briefly with Mestre Juizo. He had tricked her into making a number of strategic mistakes but she hadn't disgraced herself. As a matter of fact she had performed better than several of the senior students.

Mestre's clap on her shoulder after their play and his crisp, "Bom, Valonga," boosted her self esteem a mile high.

And after the roda, the streets, Samba-Samba-Samba from one party to another. The city was one giant dance studio. Music blared from bands parading through the main streets. Curio, Henrique, Sylvia, Sudan, Gabriela and others formed

156

the casual group that formed, dissolved and reformed on different streets, danced from one scenario to another.

They joined a large group of people dancing in the middle of the street for a half-hour . . .

"Eh!" someone shouted, "let's dance out to the beach."

She gently massaged her thighs, knees and calves. Yeahhh, that's what did me in, doing the Samba, in loose sand for four hours. She peeked at the small clock on the table next to her bed.

Ten a.m. Oh, no, it can't be that late. How will I ever make it to the Plaza for the roda? For a hard minute she seriously thought about shuffling her way back to bed and staying there until the aches went away.

"Everyone will be in the Plaza Pelourinho at noon tomorrow! All students, everybody! We are going to show the people of the city what Capoeira Angola is."

Mestre Juizo had made the announcement in Portuguese and English, for the benefit of Valonga and the three other English-speaking students in the class.

She had to be there, there was no doubt about that. The choice was simple—be in the Plaza Pelourinho at noon or run away—hide your face forever.

Mestre Juizo said noon and that means noon.

"If class is to start at 6:30 p.m., we will start at 6:30 p.m. We may begin *before* 6:330 p.m. but we will not be late to begin! Attenshun!"

She flushed the toiled and "uncurled" to a standing position.

"Ohhhhh . . ."

Maybe if I took a hot bath? She stared at the rusty faucet jutting out into the dusty tub. I guess my brain must be full of aches too.

Once again she was forced to smile at her own bad joke. The Hotel Parana had never had hot or cold running water

157

during the months she lived there. The manager made frequent promises that good things were about to happen—"Hot water for you next week, Capoeirista! Hokay?"

He called her "Capoeirista" and was always charming but none of his promises had ever been kept. Somehow it didn't really seem to matter; the hotel was centrally located, the rent was cheap and the place was filled with interesting bohemians.

Valonga uncovered the pail of water beside the tub, bending painfully to scoop a couple of large bugs out of the pail and splashed tepid water on her face. She knelt beside the pail. Hmmmmm...maybe I can make it after all, my back seems to be bending. I'll get out and have a couple cups of espresso, that should do it.

Two cups of sweet, black, steaming coffee later, she strolled through the cobblestoned streets of her neighborhood, exchanging greetings, pleasantries.

"Eh, Valonga, have you had your cafe yet?"

"I've had two cups already. And you?"

"Soon, as soon as my lazy man wakes up."

"Eh, Valonga, what time is your roda?"

"Mestre Juizo says noon."

"It will be at noon. See you there."

She loved the openness of Bahia. People laughed, cried, frowned, screamed, lived, made love, died in the middle of the street. Carnival offered a grand way of showing how it was done.

The streets were beginning to fill up once again with Carnival celebrants. The soft boom of a sensual Samba, coming from blocks away, seduced her into skipping into the heel-toe, hip-shake shoulder-arms movements of the Samba.

The stiffness and soreness began to evaporate. She could

feel the muscles in her back tingle. Samba, the healing force.

"We may be poor but thanks to the Orixa we have the Samba."

She suddenly became aware that clots of people were around her, hundreds of people swimming through the tributaries to the Plaza Pelourinho. Life was full, vivid, warm, sensuous.

The Plaza Pehourinho was filled with thousands. Valonga stood over to one side, watching the Carnival pass; a wonderful palette of people in bright colors, singing, laughing, making jokes. Women selling delicious shrimp—bean fritters from trays swaying on their heads!

I'm hungry...

She made a cross stream move to one of the vendors for two shrimp-bean fritters.

Just what I need, not too heavy.

She allowed herself to flow with the people making a clockwise motion in the plaza, enjoying the gorgeous spectacle and the delicate flavors of her fritters.

I should've gotten four of these...

11:38. Mestre Juizo said the Plaza Pelourinho. Where in the Plaza Pelourinho?

She fought down a sudden attack of anxiety. What if I can't find my school?

Ten minutes later, the insinuating tones of the berimbau pulled her toward the center of the Plaza. Of course, where else would Mestre Juizo and O Gropo Capoeira Angola be but in the center?

She ducked under the rope that cordoned off the area that they were going to play in. Two microphones, a long bench for the three berimbau players, the drummer, the pandiero, reco-reco, and agogo.

Mestre Juizo spoke to her without turning to look in her direction—"Valonga, you are not late, good. We will begin

159

in ten minutes."

Hundreds of people were already standing around the circle they were going to play in. Mestre Juizo was famous in Bahia. He was known for his serious involvement with Capoeira Angola and the superiority of his students.

Valonga exchanged greetings with her friends and began to do stretching exercises. She noticed that everyone seemed to be a bit preoccupied. Maybe it's nerves. It felt odd to have hundreds of eyes follow each movement she made. Hope I don't get stage fright.

"Valonga, did you hear?"

"Did I hear what, Sylvia?" If anybody had heard anything it would be Sylvia.

"That some Angolieros from Mestre Prakana's school will be coming here to play with us."

"It is true?"

"It's only what I heard."

The bell tone of Mestre Juizo's berimbau prevented her from asking more questions. It was time.

Thirty students wearing the black pants and green t-shirts of Mestre Juizo's school formed a two-horned circle, fifteen students on each side, the musical bench acting as the base of the horns.

They knew exactly what to do. "Each of you will go to the center, starting with the new students, perform a little ginga, do *one* movement and return to your place. The berimbau will give you the signal to begin and end."

They had rehearsed the whole thing a dozen time, Mestre Juizo was meticulous.

"Pay attenshun!"

Curio gave her the thumbs up signal as he picked up the pandiero and sat on the bench. They had an hour to perform in the hot Bahian sun.

Mestre Juizo seated himself behind the microphone at one

end of the bench, gave a nod for the other microphone to be moved near the center of the bench for the chorus.

He made a quick inventory of the musicians; he was playing the violin/solo berimbau, the person next to him the media and finally the deep throated gunga. Valonga smiled at the apple bobbing up and down in Henrique's throat.

Pandiero, atabaque, reco-reco and agogo. The Mestre spoke into the microphone.

"We are O Grupo Capoeira Angola Bahia."

The crowd roared with pleasure. Mestre Juizo was known to be a man of few words. "We are O Gropo Capoeira Angola Bahia," might have been the last sentence, after twenty minutes of speechmaking by other Mestres.

They were suddenly into it, the warm vibes of the people surrounding them, the berimbau's echoing tones, the thump of the pandiero, the first song.

Everyone knew the pecking order. The ten-year-old (Damica) darted into the center, danced his ginga a few steps and made the front-pushing kick called besoa.

Seven, eight, ten students. Now it's my turn.

Valonga felt as though she were stumbling when she danced the first steps of the ginga. The ginga was the left foot forward, alternate hand, right foot, alternate hand movement that was so simple some people found it difficult to do.

She did a simple au, a somersault, and returned to her wing, exhilarated and perspiring.

"Good, Valonga," Sudan whispered into her ear as they sang the chorus to "Eh Angola."

The preliminary over, Mestre Juizo opened the roda with a solo song about the martial art called Capoeira Angola. Valonga studied the faces of the spectators as the Mestre sang.

"This Angola is strong, sweet and can sting you. This

Angola is strong, sweet and can sting you, beware the prick of the Angoliero."

She was never certain that she understood the meanings of the Capoeira songs, they all seemed to be about one hundred more things than they were saying.

An aisle opened through the crowd at the end of the first cycle of songs and a small, muscular man about Mestre Juizo's age filed through, followed by fifteen men and women.

Valonga nodded as Sudan whispered, "Mestre Prakana, very good Angolieros, but nasty."

Capoeira Angola is the real Capoeira, Capoeira Regionale is the "created" form. The Capoeira Angola players are called Angolieros and they feel a part of the deeper tradition.

Mestre Prakana bowed to Mestre Juizo. Mestre Juizo pretended not to see Prakana or his students for a few moments.

Finally, Mestre Juizo gave Mestre Prakana a nod, motioning for him to join the roda. The Prakana school joined the Juizo school, singing choruses and clapping their hands.

Valonga thought their red t-shirts and white pants made a beautiful contrast with the Juizo green and black.

Mestre Juizo's school, host of the event, was given the right to jogo (play) with each other first.

When her turn came, Valonga squatted under the shadows of the berimbaus absentmindedly. The heat, the music, the excitement made her feel oblivious to her opponent. She focused on what she had to do to survive.

Play with the rhythm—don't do stupid things—pay attenshun!

She managed to avoid being swept to the ground by a vicious rastiera. Sudan smiled slyly at her as she used a quick au to escape the indignity of being tripped up on her back.

Chama de Magin'—meia lua—another au—rastiera.

She was grateful to hear the berimbau signal an end to her play with Sudan. She could tell from the way he shook her hand and embraced her that he, too, was pleased that their play had come to an end.

After each of the thirty members of the Juizo school had had an opportunity to have a brief play with each other, Mestre Prakana's school could join in, and they did immediately following the last play between members of the Juizo school.

The singing took on an intensity previously missing, Juizo was playing Prakana. The senior students from each school started the play.

Valonga paid automatic attention to the songs, her eyes glued to the reverence of the movements in the center of the ring.

Capoeira Angola made her feel that she was in church.

The Mae de Santos had offered her one explanation for her feelings, about Capoeira Angola . . .

"Valonga, my daughter, please understand that Capoeira Angola is the martial art of our souls, Capoeira Regional is the martial art of our bodies. Don't quote me on this, O.K.?"

It wasn't necessary to tell the people watching the play between the Prakana school and the Juizo school that something special was happening.

Most of them knew the choruses of the songs, the names of the movements, the depth of feeling that the play required.

Members of the two schools singled each other out to play with. The "play" was serious and hard.

Valonga felt an urge to be in each game, to feel the moods that the players felt.

There were times when she felt as though she was exhausted from playing a game she hadn't participated in. She felt the tap on her shoulder, as though she were in a

163

dream. One of the members of the Prakana school wanted to play with her.

She squatted in front of the berimbaus with the person who had chosen her to jogo with, waiting for the two men before them to complete their game. She made an effort not to stare into her opponent's eyes.

I don't want him to read fear in my face.

"Mestre Prakan, very good Angolieros, but nasty."

The Prakana school had a reputation for doing hard sweeps, rastieras, and for "bending" the rules of the game.

I don't care how good he is, I'm going to do the best I can. She was surprised to see Mestre Juizo smiling at her from the corner of her eye.

The two players before them concluded their game with a handshake and an embrace. Now it's my turn.

She shook hands with her opponent, staring at the ground, asked the blessing of Eshu for her game and made a slow, well-controlled au into the center.

Her opponent made a slower entrance, keeping his head and shoulders upside down, peering at her through his legs.

Valonga felt her legs weaken for a few beats after she recognized Juan rojo Diablo's face. No, it couldn't be him.

He threw a front kick to her right side, she dodged, skiva, and counter attacked with a meia lua de frente. He moved back three steps and performed the odd movement used in Capoeira Angola that signals for a little break.

She approached him cautiously as he stood with arms outstretched in a Jesus-like posture. Chamada de Magin.

Valonga stretched her arms out to meet his hands. The Chamada de Magin ("the magic walk") was three steps backward, three steps forward and a resumption of the game.

They didn't speak as they made "the magic walk" and when they resumed their play, Valonga felt a surge of energy. She attacked, he slid away from her attack and performed a monkey-drunk ginga for a few steps, something to lull her into an unguarded moment.

She wouldn't buy the trick; they exchanged knowing grins and slid to the ground for roles in opposite directions. They played beautifully together, a chess game with their bodies. If he moved directly at her, she slid off to the side. If she tried to circle him, he cut off her movement. They were playing the game the way it was supposed to be played.

For ten minutes they attacked and counter-attacked without making one obvious offensive/defensive movement. It was all mind play.

Finally, Mestre Juizo signalled with the berimbau that their play was over. The Prakana school and the Juizo school applauded their play, the crowd cheered them.

Valonga and Juan embraced, swayed against each other briefly. They had to step aside for the players of the next game.

Mestre Juizo called to Valonga from his bench. She stumbled over to him, drenched with perspiration.

"Valonga, you played well today, you can leave the roda, if you like."

"Thank you, Mestre."

There was no need to say anything else. He had read the play better than anyone in the Plaza Pelourinho.

"Thank you, Mestre."

A tight aisle opened up as she and Juan left the circle of Capoeiristas. Ten steps into the crowd they circled each others waists.

"Juan, you've made my life complete by returning to me. I never thought I'd see you again."

The wistful smile that she loved lifted the corners of his mouth.

"I had to return to you, Valonga. It would've been impossible for me to stay away from you."

The colors of the crowd, the aromas, foul and sweet, the humidity, everything seemed to be more intense. No one bumped into them, no one stared at them, it was as though they were traveling in a bubble on the ground.

"Juan, where are we going?"

"Remember where we met for the first time, the first time we made love?"

"Yes, on the banks of a river, where I went with Malana."

"Yes, on the banks of the Black Grass river, where everything is beautiful and in harmony. That's where I live, that's where I want to take you."

"When do we leave?"

"We're on our way now..."